MT W
steelma

D0757971

THE GREAT YELLOWSTONE STEAMBOAT RACE

THE GREAT
YELLOWSTONE
STEAMBOAT RACE

Robert J. Steelman

GUNSMOKE

First published in the US by Doubleday

This hardback edition 2013
by AudioGO Ltd
by arrangement with
Golden West Literary Agency

ISBN 978 1 471 32129 0

British Library Cataloguing in Publication Data available.

Printed and bound in Great Britain by
MPG Books Group Limited

"Its draft was so slight that one humorist described the vessel as being '. . . . so built that when the river is low and the sandbars come out for air, the first mate can tap a keg of beer and run four miles on the suds.'"

The Rivermen (The Old West)

New York, Time-Life Books, 1975

Robert J. Steelman was born in Columbus, Ohio. He graduated from Ohio State University in 1938 and worked for thirty years as an electronics engineer before he retired and devoted himself solely to writing novels, although in the early 1950s he had already contributed Western short stories to pulp magazines, such as the excellent "Medicine Man Magic" in *Ranch Romances* (1st November Number: 11/6/53). *Stages South* (Ace, 1956) was his first published novel, a story concerning the attempt by the Confederacy to seize the Overland Stage Line. Steelman once commented: "My writing is largely of the Old West. I try hard to make my books authoritative and true to the times. Perhaps my principal aim is to do what I can to elevate the 'Western' to some literary significance, rather than see it condemned to a second-rate genre status." This literary skill certainly is on display in his Western novels that often have American Indian themes like *Winter of the Sioux* (Doubleday, 1959) and Lord Apache (Doubleday, 1977). Particularly noteworthy among his consistently fine Westerns would be *Portrait of a Sioux* (Doubleday, 1976), a story about an ex-scout who is persuaded by a rich widow from the East to take her into the heart of Sioux territory so she can persuade Sans Arc Chief Walking Bull to sit for a portrait, or *The Great Yellowstone Steamboat Race* (Doubleday, 1980). In his later novels Steelman added humor to what are essentially serious themes, as in *The Holdout* (Walker, 1984), with its unlikely hero, Charlie Calloway, a draft-dodging gambler and former dentist, an obvious take off on the historical Doc Holliday. At its best Steelman's Western fiction is lucid, experimental, entertaining, and always informed by historical accuracy.

Chapter One

There were two flood seasons on the Upper Missouri and the Yellowstone. The April rise was caused by the melting of prairie snows. The larger June rise came when mountain snowmelt reached low ground. The latter, along with the remnants of the April rise, made of the rivers a muddy torrent. At Springer's Landing, near the confluence of the two rivers, the high water was at its worst. Tied up to the docks with stout hawsers fore and aft were the *Sultan*, flagship of Missouri Packet Lines, along with the shabby independents, *Rambler*, *General Dixon*, *Eclipse*, *Firefly*, *Pioneer*, *Acme*, and *Dauntless*. Later on, when the waters abated, they would make considerable profit carrying freight and passengers upstream and down, to army posts, straggling river towns, the gold diggings —wherever a river steamer could nose in to a reed-bordered shore and swing out the gangplank; the Mauvaises Terres, Fort Mahone, Musselshell City, Camp Cooke, the Lucky Lady mine, the Cheyenne Agency on Cherry Creek, Bismarck, and Yankton. Now they waited. Captains cursed; the pilots, on salary, played poker in the Paradise Saloon; owners bewailed continuing rains that pushed sailing dates later and later into the summer.

On Wicket's Branch, a sizable stream emptying into the Upper Missouri near Springer's Landing, one vessel was tied up more securely than the others. Restlessly the *Rose of Dundee* moved at her moorings. In addition to the tattered hawsers securing her, an iron chain with a large brass padlock draped from her bow to an oak tree at the water's edge. Sheriff Ben Bagley owned the key to the padlock. To the pilothouse door was tacked a document attaching the *Rose of Dundee* until her master's debt of three hundred and fifty dollars to the Tobin Marine Works was paid in full.

"There!" Uncle Hugh Munro said, extending a tin dipper of whisky toward his nephew, Alec. "Try that, now, boyo, and see if Munro's Highland Elixir appeals to you!"

Alec Munro, master and pilot of the *Rose of Dundee*, was a tall and rawboned young man with a shock of dark hair, melancholy blue eyes, and a week's growth of beard. Sitting in a sag-bottomed wicker chair under the shelter of the hurricane deck, he laid down a copy of Plutarch's *Lives* and sipped gingerly.

"Better," he admitted. "Still got a taste of engine oil to her, though."

Hugh Munro, chief and only engineer of the imprisoned *Rose of Dundee,* was a small man in singlet and tattered pants, looking like an ancient Skye terrier, even to a grayness around the muzzle. He tasted the brew himself, wiped his whiskered mouth with a sleeve. "You're right," he admitted. "When I put that new condensing coil on the still I didn't clean her out too good first." He spat, threw the contents of the dipper over the side.

Cupping his hands, Alec yelled after Hugh, who was scurrying aft to the engine room. "Stop using up our cordwood to fire that damned still! We couldn't get up enough steam to blow your nose with the bit of kindling that's left!"

In the lee of the now-cold boiler squatted Alec's seven slippered and skull-capped Chinese deckhands, leftovers from the building of a railroad which had gotten as far as Fort Wadsworth on the Dakota River and expired from an embezzlement of funds. Uncle Hugh communicated with the Chinese in some mysterious way, he in Gaelic and they in Cantonese, although they only gazed blankly at Alec. Sam Fat, the leader, crouched over a charcoal brazier cooking something in a pot. The rest, pigtails dangling, crowded about. Boiled muskrat,

Alec decided; he had not been able to pay them for weeks, but the Orientals had no other place to go.

In drumming rain he walked from under the hurricane deck to the forward capstan, looking lovingly back at his sweetheart. Rosie was small, compared to Missouri Packet boats like the *Sultan,* but stouthearted and willing. With her spoonlike bow Rosie could carry two hundred tons upriver at five knots—double that if another foot of draft could be tolerated over her normal thirty inches. The main deck was open-sided, housing the firebox, open to the front for better draft, the boiler, the engine, the cargo, and whatever deck passengers bought passage. Hog chains ran fore and aft over a high support to brace her keel against sagging. Forward was mounted the small brass cannon, loaded with boiler rivets to repel Indian attacks. The single-cylinder, high-pressure engine was installed on its side and connected to the stern paddle wheel by a long ironbound log, the "pitman." Ranged along the gunwales were dozens of wooden barrels for boiler water. The Yellowstone was muddy, each bucket containing a double handful of silt and sand. Good captains let water from the river first settle in barrels filled with prickly pear, the cactus acting as a kind of filter.

From Rosie's main deck there rose, near the capstan, two oak spars; their butt ends were secured on the deck and they were supported vertically by rope stays. Forty feet long, in their upright position even higher than the stacks, they weighed several hundred pounds each. In slack water they were used for "grasshoppering"; when Rosie stranded on a bar, they were lowered butt-first into the river. By a system of ropes and pulleys powered by the forward capstan they could be employed like a pair of giant crutches to pull the boat forward and upward.

On Rosie's noble summit sat the pilothouse, sheathed in boiler plate against Indian attack and adorned by a polished brass plate carrying her name. If Alec ever came into money, he would have the roof sheathed also in boiler plate. Last sea-son the pesky Indians had learned that the roof was vulnerable, and had favored ambushes from the bluffs where they could shoot arrows and bullets downward. The Sioux, particularly, were wily. Since many of the woodyards along the river were run by tame Indians, old Bad Eye and his Sioux brothers frequently took them over, ambushing unwary captains. Still, with all the perils and dangers, Alec longed to be steaming upriver now with a full deckload, the cranky high-pressure engine exhausting like a cannonade. Even in this high water he dared go. He was a lightning pilot; the deer antlers on the pilothouse were a badge of skill. But now—

Damp and dismal, he retreated under the rain-drumming shelter of the hurricane deck to watch a wagon train wind across the wooden bridge spanning Wicket's Branch. They had come up the old Military Road from the east and Alec wondered how they had ever gotten this far, with the rain turning Territory roads into a quagmire.

Beside the driver of the lead wagon sat an erect military figure, swathed in an army waterproof and wearing a black Kossuth hat looped up on the side in cavalry style. Alec, once corporal in the Iron Brigade at Gettysburg, recognized the gold cord, tipped with acorns, of an officer.

From the high seat the man cupped his hands and yelled, "Who runs things around here?"

Alec, no favorite with officers during his military experience, only glowered at the wagon and resumed whittling.

Exasperated, the officer climbed down and approached, carrying a carbine. He was a stocky, square-cut man with extravagantly waxed mustachios and small bright eyes, like a ferret.

"Look here!" he said impatiently. "My name's Gamble, Rollo P. Gamble—lieutenant, Third Cavalry, assistant quartermaster at Fort Van Buren in Dakota, formerly on General Sherman's staff at the Department of the Missouri. I'm on an important mission and need cooperation from the civil authorities."

Alec stood, brushed shavings from his jeans. "I guess you

better go up the hill and talk to Horace Tobin." He pointed through slanting sheets of rain to the white house with the veranda that topped the bluff overlooking Springer's Landing.

"Tobin?" Lieutenant Gamble made a sudden entry in a notebook. He moved quickly and decisively, also like a ferret.

"Horace runs the Tobin Marine Works—you can see their ways on the side of the hill. Tobin's mayor of the town, owns most of the property hereabouts, along with the majority of Missouri Packet Lines stock."

Horace Tobin was Nora Tobin's father, though Alec did not think Lieutenant Gamble would be interested. How an ugly old man like Horace, with a perpetual scowl framed by massive side-whiskers, could sire such a beautiful daughter was a mystery.

"Thanks!" Gamble said, closing the notebook. "Carry on!"

Involuntarily, Alec said, "Yes, sir." Then, annoyed at being tricked into military ways again, he climbed the ladder to let himself into his dank and gloomy pilothouse. Damned shoulderboards!

Sitting on the stool before the oaken wheel, he counted the money in the battered tin box. Seventy-six, seventy-seven, seventy-eight—seventy-eight dollars and a handful of change. And he was in debt to old Tobin for three hundred and fifty dollars! Putting the money back into the box, he slid it into a drawer. Sadly he rubbed the worn oak of the wheel, polished the brass hub with his sleeve. "Rosie," he murmured. "Ah, Rosie! Whatever shall we do?"

On the grassy banks of the creek the teamsters pulled up their wagons and rigged a canvas shelter under which they squatted around a fire. Some played cards, others drank from flasks and stone bottles. One man broiled a chunk of meat on a willow twig. A cat meowed; probably a mule skinner's pet. Alec jumped when the door banged. Uncle Hugh came in with a fresh dipperful of Munro's Highland Elixir. "I think I've got it now!" he announced. "Try this!"

It didn't have the smoky tang of the genuine article from

Morgan's Distillery on the banks of Loch Tay, but made up for the lack of smoke with an abundance of fire. Hugh's latest effort burned all the way down.

"I guess it'll do," Alec muttered.

His uncle peered at him. "You down in the mouth again, boyo?"

"What else would a man be, a great debt lying on his shoulders like a cross, and going to lose his livelihood at sheriff's sale?" Alec clenched his fist, shook it at Horace Tobin's great house. "That cursed old man will buy Rosie for a nickel on the dollar and paint her in Missouri Packet colors! He'll make a gaudy whore out of Rosie, like his other boats!" Agitated, he paced the cabin. "Before I see her brought down like that, uncle, I'll burn her to the water's edge!"

Hugh shook a finger. "Now let's not be talking of burning our own flesh and blood! Things will turn out all right, you'll see." His face brightened at the sight of the teamsters under the canvas shelter. "If you could let me have a few dollars from that tin box, I could join those ruffians in their gambling and win us a big pot."

"Not on your life! That's all the money we've got in the world!"

"But—"

"No buts!"

"Well," Hugh grumbled, "there's no need to scream at me— your father's best-loved brother!" He gestured with the dipper at the Tobin house. "Don't think I don't know what's *really* eating at you!"

"What is it you're hinting at?"

"Nora Tobin going to marry Julius Winkle! That's what's put you in an ugly state! By the blessed waters of Loch Tay, you'd let our poor old Rosie go by the boards while you moon over a lost love!"

Alec was indignant. "I never loved Nora Tobin!"

"Swith, and you did, you stubborn Scot!"

"How could I be jealous of that fop and fool of a Winkle?

Didn't he blow his boiler at Waterman's Bar last summer trying to catch us and we had to tow him? Why, old Rosie made Missouri Packet Lines the laughingstock of the Yellowstone!"

"Foosh!" Uncle Hugh cried. "I know the contrary hearts of Munro men! Your father was the same way with the females—cold as a clam outside while his heart burned with passion! Well, you'll not catch Nora Tobin that way, nephew!"

"I don't love Nora Tobin! Her eyes are too big, and her mouth a trifle wide. Anyway, when she came back from Miss Waddell's Female Seminary in Omaha she was too damned refined for me! That way of sticking her little finger up in the air when she drinks tea, and talking through her nose! She never *used* to be that way! Why, I remember when we—when we—"

He broke off, remembering happier days when the *Rose of Dundee* plied the Yellowstone, decks loaded with paying cargo and passengers. Always Alec had looked forward to tying up at Springer's Landing, seeing Nora again. That was before Nora went away to Miss Waddell's. Summer, he remembered—a dinghy drifting aimlessly on the still waters of Wicket's Branch, Nora picking wildflowers from the bank. He watched her bare brown arms, the cleft in her chin, cast covert glances at the high bosom under the lace ruching. Nora, he thought, heart pierced with pain. *Rosie—and Nora. Lost, forever lost!*

"You mope around like you were in a trance! A man talks to you, and you're away on the moon!" Hugh dangled a gold watch before Alec. "Your father left me this timepiece and I'd as soon part with it as my right arm! But we need cash, Alec! If you won't give me any money, I'll hock this precious memento! I'm going in to the Paradise Saloon and join the stud poker game."

"Good luck." Alec shrugged.

It continued to rain. The river rose higher, threatening to sweep away the pilings on which half the town of Springer's Landing was built. Preparations went on in the Tobin house for a grand party, with champagne from St. Louis, to announce the engagement of Nora Tobin to Julius Winkle, master of the *Sultan*, Missouri Packet's flagship. Lieutenant Rollo P. Gamble came and went on mysterious errands while his teamsters continued to gamble, drink, and fight alongside the *Rose of Dundee*. Uncle Hugh Munro lost the gold watch to Woolly Willie Yates.

"He's a skunk!" Uncle Hugh grumbled.

"Who?"

"Willie! Woolly Willie! That man is too lucky by half! I was ahead thirty-seven dollars and sixty cents when he sprung those three sevens on me! It makes a man wonder!"

"If I were you," Alec warned, "I wouldn't wonder too much! Willie's a lot bigger than you, and twice as ugly. They say he killed a grizzly once with his bare hands."

"Nevertheless, I'll fix his clock! It isn't natural for a man to come up with three of a kind that often!"

"Look!" Alec said. "Here comes shoulderboards Gumble, or Gamble, or whatever his name is, with his moustache waxed fit to stab someone."

In the growing dusk Lieutenant Rollo P. Gamble stamped up the gangplank.

"Dolts!" he snapped. "Fools! Cowards!"

They stared at him.

"Not you," Gamble apologized. He tugged hard at the moustaches. "Them!" He swept his arm toward the paddlewheelers in serried ranks along the wharves. "There isn't a man among those captains! That's why I've come to you, Mr. Munro." He swept off the dramatic Kossuth hat and slapped his thigh. "A soldier's got to follow orders—right?"

"I guess so."

"There's a combined military movement scheduled for the twelfth of June. Never mind its nature—that's a military secret! But the purpose is to catch the damned Sioux between three columns, and settle their hash for once and for all. Now I've got seventeen wagons full of supplies for Fort Mahone, sup-

plies essential for that operation. But we're way behind sched-
ule already! What with the mud and all, we'll never make Fort
Mahone in time!"

Alec scratched a bristled chin. "How does that concern me?"

Gamble spat into Wicket's Branch. "The roads are so bad
that my only chance to get those supplies to Fort Mahone is to
take them upriver on a paddle-wheeler. Julius Winkle and the
rest of those lily-livered scoundrels won't run the river in this
condition! They fear for their vessels! They say, 'Wait a week
or so and see what the river does!' Well, by God, I can't wait,
and neither can General Terry! There'll be hell to pay in the
War Department if those supplies don't get to Fort Mahone by
the twelfth of this month!"

Seeing Gamble's agitation, Uncle Hugh poured him a tin
cup of the Elixir.

"What's that?" Gamble asked, peering into the cup.

"Just a little *usquebaugh*," Uncle Hugh said. "It will calm
your nerves."

"You're the best pilot on the river," Gamble went on. He
coughed, blew his nose, drank the whisky down. "Some, like
that fat Julius Winkle, don't agree. But the general consensus
is there's only one man can take a paddle-wheeler up the
Yellowstone this time of year. That's you!"

Alec laughed, mirthlessly.

"I know, I know!" Gamble agreed. "Good God, what's this
sludge in the bottom of my cup? Anyway, I'm familiar with
your financial troubles. So I had an idea. Your boat's chained
up here, attached by the sheriff. Tell you what we'll do! We'll
go together up to Tobin's place and make him a proposition.
If he'll agree to release you from that writ of attachment, we'll
load my supplies onto the *Rose of Dundee* and steam up to
Fort Mahone—if you're game, that is. Then I'll authorize payment to you of five hundred dollars. You can settle your debt
with Tobin, get your boat back, and have money left over!"

Alec blinked. The idea was attractive. "Pour me some of
that witch's brew," he instructed Hugh.

"Alec," Uncle Hugh complained, "no one has ever seen the Yellowstone this high!"

Alec took a mouthful of the Elixir, contemplating Gamble's offer.

"Are you scared too?" Gamble demanded.

"I'm scared!" Uncle Hugh confessed. "Alec, think this over before you kill old Rosie on a snag!"

Alec thought of *Rose of Dundee* in Missouri Packet colors, flying the Missouri Packet Lines house flag. He couldn't abide that—never! Better let her go to the bottom honorably, pierced by a sawyer, than enter into a life of whoredom with Horace Tobin!

"Lieutenant," he decided, "I accept your offer." Taking a lantern from a locker, he lit it and turned up the wick. "It's getting dark," he said. "Let's go! You too, uncle—we're partners."

"Not me!" Uncle Hugh protested. "I've got more productive things to do with my time than go begging to Horace Tobin!"

"And what, pray tell, would that be?"

Hugh ignored the question. "You well know, nephew, Horace Tobin has a heart tough as a hickory nut, and several times smaller! He'd not give you the trimmings from his beard!"

"All right," Alec shrugged. "Do as you like, you stubborn old man!" Nodding to Lieutenant Gamble, he held the lamp high to illuminate their way through the rain. "Come on!"

The Tobin mansion blazed with lamps and candles for the engagement party. Everyone in Springer's Landing seemed to have been invited, along with captains, mates, and pursers of the boats. The graveled drive before the pillared veranda was crowded with springwagons and buckboards. Horses with rain-wet saddles were tied to the long hitching post, roofed with tin against summer heat and winter snows. Inside, a scratchy fiddle and a banjo played "Come Where My Love Lies Dreaming." Alec knocked at the door, multicolored glass panels set in lead to a fair approximation of a draped maiden bending over a forest pool. Bessie, the Tobins' black maid, came to the door in an unaccustomed starched pinafore, white cap pinned to her kinky curls.

"Mr. Alec!"

"Hello, Bessie," he said. "I'd like to see Mr. Tobin."

Bessie's black face wrinkled in concern. "You ain't invited, Mr. Alec. Them's hard lines, but—"

"It's all right," Alec said, pushing by her and wringing out his rain-soaked nautical cap in the umbrella-stand. "This is business."

Twisting the dank hat, he stopped. Nora Tobin stood in the doorway leading to the parlor; from beyond her drifted sounds of revelry.

"Alec!" she said in surprise.

"It's me," he admitted. Awkwardly he turned. "This is Lieutenant Gamble, from Fort Van Buren, in Dakota."

He had to admit that Nora was magnificently turned out. From long absence in Omaha she had lost the sun-browned skin, the boyish ways. Now, in a clinging white gown spattered with sequins, taffy-colored hair piled atop her head in wavelets held in place by jeweled combs, face pale with powder but full lips red and pouting, she sidled toward them, waving her fan.

"We—we're here on business," Alec stammered. "Nothing to do with—with—" He swallowed, inclined his head toward the parlor. "Nothing to do with your party."

Gentian-blue eyes regarding him strangely, she waved the fan, wafting toward him the scent of French perfume. Nora had never smelled like that before—had never looked like this before, either. Then she smiled. "Lieutenant Gamble, I am happy to make your acquaintance!"

Gamble stepped forward with a flourish and took her hand, kissing it. "Your servant, ma'am."

Nora's blue eyes widened. "What a pleasure to meet a man of culture and refinement in these rude surroundings!"

Alec shifted his feet. "Nora, it's business we're about, business with your father. Can we see him?"

Nora blinked, moved her head slightly in the direction of the doorway of Horace Tobin's library, off the hallway. Was she trying to tell him something?

"Bessie, please go upstairs to the front sitting room where Father and the other gentlemen are. Tell him Mr. Alec and a Lieutenant Gamble are here to see him on business." To Gamble she said, "Sir, will you excuse us for a moment? I have something to say to Mr. Munro."

Gamble bowed again; he did it expertly, Alec thought. Nora drew Alec into the darkened library, closing the door so that only a thin bar of light showed. The powdered face glimmered white; too much powder, Alec thought. Before, Nora had always scoffed at female vanities.

"You're such a goose!" she hissed. "Alec, you embarrassed me dreadfully! Didn't you see me winking to attract your attention?"

"I thought—"

"It was always hard to attract your attention! I mean—attract you in a way that—that—"

"I don't know what you mean," he protested. "After all, how was I to know?"

"Oh, pooh!" Nora declared, sending out a perfect gale with her fan. "I declare I—I simply can't—" She folded the fan. "You know I'm going to be engaged to Julius Winkle."

He stood dumbly by her, uneasy at the heady French scent, more accustomed to engine oil, steam, and muddy water.

"It's a good match. I mean—don't you think so? After all, Julius is senior captain on the line, and a stockholder, too. His prospects are good to be commodore some day, Father says."

"What do I care about you and Julius Winkle? I wouldn't even have come up here if it hadn't had to do with business!" Alec folded his arms to justify a little more distance between them. "I certainly wasn't invited!"

She had a quick temper, but bit her tongue.

"Of course you weren't invited! After all—with what we'd

been to each other! Like the French say, it wasn't *comme il faut* to ask you to my engagement party!"

"I don't know any French," he muttered. "Only Gaelic. Anyway, we were never really anything to each other. It was just a passing affair!"

In the thin slit of light he saw a glint of moisture in her eye. "If you take a rolled-up corner of a handkerchief and poke it around in the corner of your eye," he advised, "it'll catch that cinder or whatever it is. Now I have to go, Nora."

"Alec, wait!"

He turned, hand on the brass doorknob.

"Why do you have to be so stiff and all?"

"I'm not stiff!" he lied. He was so stiff and tight he feared he might be coming apart all at once, like a spring-wound toy cranked too far.

"I only wanted to talk to you once more!"

"There's nothing to talk about," he said. "I wish you a happy marriage and lots of children." Mentally he quailed at the image of a band of small Julius Winkles at her knee. "I really do, Nora!"

The quaver in her voice should have warned him. When Nora was angry she tended to rush about a great deal and swear, though perhaps she had lost that facility at Miss Waddell's.

"You're a damned liar!" she cried. "Alec, why do you play with me this way? Here I'm going to marry a man that can give me comfort and security and position, and all you do is say nasty things!"

"So that's the way it is!" he said triumphantly. "Comfort, security, position, when all I've got is *Rose of Dundee,* that looks like a teapot on a shingle compared to Winkle's *Sultan!* You didn't used to turn up your nose at me and Rosie! Well, let me tell you, my fine lady—Rosie's a better and a faster boat than Winkle's *Sultan* any day! And I'm a better man than Julius Winkle at any game you want to play!"

"Oh, no, you're not!" Nora cried. "Julius makes me feel

like a woman, not a fishing companion! Julius says nice things to me, brings me presents, courted me proper! All you ever did was treat me like a boy, talk about boiler rivets and oak cordwood and paddle-dips per minute! That's no way to treat a girl—I mean a *woman!*"

Suddenly contrite, he reached for her hand. But now she was the one who drew away. She wept into her lace handkerchief. He realized this time that they were real tears, not just something in her eye.

"Listen," he begged. "Listen, Nora! I'm sorry, but—"

"Oh, go away!" she sobbed. "You don't understand anything, Alec! You never did!"

There was a discreet knock at the door. Rollo Gamble stood in the hallway, whistling negligently. The fiddle and banjo were playing. *My true love is a blue-eyed daisy. If I don't get her I'll go crazy.*

"Let's go up," Alec said.

In the grand parlor the Turkey carpets had been taken up and the guests were dancing a schottische. As Bessie escorted them up the grand staircase, Gamble whispered in Alec's ear. "What was Miss Tobin crying about?"

"How the hell would I know?" Alec snapped.

In the second-floor sitting room old Horace had his office. Now he sat drinking bourbon with cronies—Julius Winkle and Sheriff Ben Bagley. Alec and Lieutenant Gamble stood at the edge of the circle of lamplight.

"I hear you wanted to see me, Alec," old Horace said.

For all that he had padlocked the *Rose of Dundee,* Ben Bagley had been Alec's friend. Maybe that was what made him such a good sheriff; Ben managed to remain friends even with the miscreants confined in his jail.

Julius Winkle said nothing. Sleek in his tailor-made uniform, he regarded Alec Munro with distaste, heavy-lidded eyes half closed.

"This is Lieutenant Rollo Gamble," Alec explained, "from

down at Fort Van Buren. He's got a consignment of military stores that must get up to Fort Mahone by the twelfth of this month."

"I've heard all that," Horace Tobin grunted. "And here you are again, Lieutenant."

"Yes, sir," Gamble admitted, flushing, "only this time I have a different proposition."

"That so?"

"As you know, sir, I had no success persuading any of the valiant river captains to forward my supplies."

Julius Winkle sighed delicately. "The river is very high!"

"I learned there was one real pilot left on the river." Gamble nodded toward Alec. "The trouble is, you've got Captain Munro's *Lily of the Valley*—"

"*Rose of Dundee!*" Alec corrected.

"You've got his vessel attached for debt."

"That's right," Horace Tobin agreed. "Munro owes me three hundred and fifty dollars for repairs to her bottom, and I *need* that money! Can't imagine how much it takes to marry off a daughter in proper style!"

"Sir!" Gamble said. "If you'll release Munro from the writ of attachment, we'll load my freight onto the *Rose of Machree*—"

"*Dundee!*" Alec objected. "*Rose of Dundee!* You ought to learn her name! She's the fastest boat on the river!"

"Except the *Sultan*, perhaps," Julius Winkle murmured silkily.

Disregarding interruptions, Lieutenant Gamble went on.

"Captain Munro will get me out of this fix and I'll pay him five hundred dollars freight charges. A little high, maybe, but in view of the emergency, justified. Then he can pay you back."

Horace Tobin's eyes narrowed. "Cash?"

"Cash?"

"On the barrelhead!"

"I haven't got a cent! I had to pay off those damned teamsters when they got surly down the road a ways! But when we get to Fort Mahone I'll have the post quartermaster issue a purchase order."

Tobin shook his grizzled head. "No deal! Do you take me for an idiot? That relic of Alec Munro's will capsize in this floodwater! You'll lose your precious freight, Gamble, and I'll lose my lawful security on his debt! No, sir—I didn't get where I am today by entertaining harebrained notions! Now if you're through talking nonsense, you'll have to excuse me. I've got guests downstairs, and an important announcement concerning my daughter Nora and Captain Winkle here." He rose, fixing them with a baleful stare. Julius Winkle smiled a sly smile.

"I'm afraid you still don't understand, sir!" Gamble said stiffly. "This operation is being watched personally by the Secretary of War!"

"And I'm being watched by the stockholders of Missouri Packet Lines, which includes large amounts of widows and orphans!"

"There will be repercussions in the matter of government contracts to your vessels!" Gamble warned.

Tobin's side-whiskers stood out as if under an electrical discharge. His wattles turned pink, then mottled purple. "At that time," he thundered, "you may expect repercussions from my friend Senator Claibourne of the Armed Forces Committee in Congress! So do not threaten me further!"

Alec took Gamble by the arm. "No use talking any more! Come along!"

On the landing outside, Sheriff Bagley caught up with Alec. "Son," he said, "I'm sorry Horace was so hard on you and your friend. Still, he's got a point, you know—the river so high and all." He went with Alec down the grand staircase. "But don't do anything rash, now! I know you; you didn't get that reputation on the river by being a milksop!"

Alec set his jaw. "That old man wants Rosie, and he's not going to get her, Ben!"

Bessie showed them out. "You're going to catch your death of cold, Mr. Alec!" she protested. "Here—wait a minute till I swipe one of the umbrellas in the stand! They don't need *that* many!"

"Thanks, Bessie," Alec said wearily, putting on the sodden uniform cap with CAPTAIN worked above the visor in bedraggled gold braid. "I'm all right."

The black woman remained on the veranda, watching in concern, as they walked across the wet gravel of the carriageway and paused in the shelter of the tin-roofed hitching post. The fiddle and banjo were playing again. *My true love is a blue-eyed daisy*.

"God damn!" Gamble exploded. "I've got a mind to commandeer his boat in spite of them! The general would back me up, I know! It'd mean putting my career on the line, but—"

"Wait a minute!"

"Eh?" The rain had done in Gamble's waxed moustaches; they sagged dismally. "What's on your mind?"

"We didn't lose yet!"

"How so?"

"We'll off-load your freight onto Rosie and make a flat shirttail out of here! She's tied up far enough upstream so with the rain and the noise of the river they'll never hear us till it's too late!"

Gamble shook his head. "I can't ask you to do that! Remember that writ on the pilothouse door? And what about the chain on the keel or whatever you call the front end of a boat?"

"Damn the writ!" Alec shouted. "Damn the chain! A few minutes' work with a maul and I'll smash the padlock!"

"Not so loud! Do you want everyone in the house to hear you? If the U. S. Army's going to be accessory to a crime I'd rather you didn't shout it all over the Territory!"

For the first time since Rosie had been jailed, Alec felt light and gay, refreshed.

"Light a shuck!" he urged Gamble, hurrying from the shelter. "We've got to wake up those drunken mule skinners and get them busy loading freight!"

Chapter Two

When they returned to *Rose of Dundee* the rain had stopped.
In its place was a thick fog. They groped their way through
the clinging stuff, guided by the glow from a lamp in the
pilothouse. Rollo Gamble hurried to rouse the sleeping
teamsters. Alec found a sledge and hefted it to his shoulder.

"Where's Uncle Hugh?" he asked a drowsy Chinese.

The man, raising his head from a burlap sack on which he
was huddled, stared at him, sickly sweet fumes of opium curling from his pipe.

"Uncle Hugh!" Alec pantomimed raising a bottle to his lips.
"My uncle! The smelly old man that runs the engine!"

Only blankness—but the man said something in singsong
Cantonese and Sam Fat shuffled up in felt slippers.

"Uncle Hugh, Sam Fat! Where in perdition is he?"

Sam Fat was a good river man, though he feared dragons
that he claimed lived in the Yellowstone and emerged at night
to eat people. Since he performed the function of mud clerk on
the *Rose of Dundee* as well as many other duties—cook, bos'n,
oiler, and junior pilot—Alec added, "Tally in that freight that's
coming alongside! We're taking a full cargo upstream to Fort
Mahone!"

Sam Fat's slanted eyes goggled at the boxes and sacks and
barrels being carried up the gangplank, then looked at the
dark river. "You crazy, Cap?"

Alec started toward the shore end of the chain with his
sledge. "No, I'm not crazy! Rouse up Uncle Hugh and—"

"He not here," Sam Fat said, tucking hands into capacious
sleeves.

"Not here?" Alec's mouth dropped open. "Where in hell is he?"

Sam Fat looked inscrutable. He and Uncle Hugh Munro were bosom companions; Hugh occasionally distilled for him a fiery rice wine called *ng ka py*. "Do' know."

Hefting the sledge, Alec retraced his steps. "Before I crush your heathen skull, where is Hugh Munro?"

Sam Fat retreated, fumbling nervously with his pigtail. "Go play poker," he quavered. "Long time ago!"

"Poker? But he didn't have a cent! Why in the world would he—" Alec felt a chill seep into his stomach. Hurrying up the ladder to the pilothouse, he opened the tin box. The seventy-eight dollars in bills was gone. All that remained was the handful of loose change.

"The old fool!" he gritted between clenched teeth. Now he remembered Hugh's cryptic words when Alec and Rollo Gamble left the boat. *I've got more productive things to do with my time than go begging to Horace Tobin!*

He turned as Gamble entered the pilothouse.

"Shouldn't you be getting up steam or whatever it is you do on a boat?" Gamble had regained some of his briskness, but seeing the gloom on Alec's face he left off trying to repair his sodden moustaches. "Nothing wrong, is there?"

Alec closed the tin box, put it in the drawer, slammed the drawer shut. "It's a family affair," he muttered, and hurried down the ladder.

"Sam Fat," he ordered, "stoke up the fires! Then send one of your boys into Springer's Landing chop-chop—you understand? I want him to look through all the saloons and brothels till he finds Hugh Munro, and bring him back here if he has to stuff him in a gunnysack! We're weighing anchor at first light and Hugh is the only man on the river can make that blasted engine run!"

Seeing his supply of *ng ka py* imperiled, Sam Fat quailed. "He tell me no snitch, Cap!" But in response to Alec's determined gesture with the sledge, Sam capitulated. He crooked a finger, and one of the coolies shuffled forward.

"Not him!" Alec objected. "Send that big one over there—the mean-looking one!"

But as the Chinese trotted down the gangplank, Hugh Munro burst from the bushes along the bank. Looking fearfully behind him, he scampered up the gangplank. When he saw Alec's baleful glare, he paused, uncertain. Taking a wad of waste from his pocket, he mopped his brow.

"Good morning, all!" he ventured.

"Where the hell have you been?"

"Alec," Uncle Hugh said, sidling forward, "I can explain everything, dear boy!"

"I'm not your dear boy!" Alec picked up the sledge. "But do come over here, uncle, and tell me all about it!"

Hugh wet his lips, kept a distance. "Ah—it was a nice night for a stroll, and I—"

"It was raining!"

"Well, then, all was so fresh and green—nightbirds calling to their mates, and the smell of blossoming things, just like Loch Tay in springtime—"

Under the obsidian stare he broke off; the pink tongue emerged again from the whiskers to lick his lips.

"Where's the money?"

Hugh hung his head, clasped hands before him in saintly resignation. "Swith, I heard a call from the Lord, the Presbyterian one! He told me if I'd take that money and go into town, I could double it—nay, triple it—before sunup. I wanted to pay off our debt, you understand. But somehow I seem to have fallen from grace." He shuffled his feet, examined the greasy bosom of the singlet. "I lost it!"

"Lost it?"

"Every last dollar. Nephew, I'm sorry, but—"

Alec prowled toward him with the sledge. Rollo Gamble, fearing bloodshed, pulled him back.

"All of it?" Alec demanded.

Hugh nodded, solemnly. "I've sinned, Alec, so I've decided to go off among the Indians and do good works the rest of my days." Hands still clasped in supplication, he spoke cautiously to Lieutenant Gamble. "Take hold of that coattail a little tighter, if you please! He's slipping."

"Hugh Munro, you old sinner, I ought to tie a grate bar around your neck and drop you over the side!"

Hugh looked soulful. "I understand how you feel, nephew," he said. "Now I'll just be off to do my work among the Sioux, and—"

"Look to the engine!" Alec snarled. "As soon as we get loaded we're going to back down the Branch and get underway!"

"What about my good works among the Sioux?"

Alec started toward him with the sledge, but Hugh scuttled out of his way, running toward the engine room aft. Sledge in hand, Alec then remembered what he had started out to do and immediately dispatched Ben Bagley's padlock with a few deft swings, listening with pleasure as the brass fragments and part of the chain dropped into Wicket's Branch. "Well done!" Gamble applauded. "I like your style with that sledge!"

Loading a hundred tons of cargo took longer than Alec had figured. It was near dawn when it was all aboard and suitably piled, stowed, and lashed. Followed by Gamble, he finally hurried up the ladder to the pilothouse and shouted to Sam Fat through his speaking trumpet. "Swing in the gangplank! Cast off the after lines! Cast off the bow lines!"

As *Rose of Dundee* drifted away from the bank, moving backward down Wicket's Branch, Alec spun the wheel, looking into a low ground fog illumined by a murky dawn. On shore the mule skinners cheered and waved their hats. Glowing cinders poured in sheets from the stacks, and blazing brands fell on deck while Sam Fat's gang shoved wood into the firebox. Gamble held tightly to a stanchion.

"Give me fifteen revolutions!" Alec called into the speaking tube that led to the engine room.

Now they were backing into the main current of the flooded Yellowstone. The stern-wheeler heeled violently, slewed around. From somewhere below a leaky steam line roared, sending a cloud of vapor into the pilothouse. Gamble paled and clung tighter to the stanchion.

"Did something blow up?"

Alec shook his head and turned the wheel to starboard. "All river steamers are a little limber. When the current catches Rosie, she bends a mite, and the steam fittings loosen. Nothing, nothing at all!" He clung with one hand to the binnacle as Rosie swirled like a child's toy in the mainstream. "Now!" he shouted into the speaking tube. "Give me twenty ahead, Hugh! Quick!"

For a moment *Rose of Dundee* hesitated, heeling far over like a racing schooner. The stern wheel lifted partway from the water; the engine raced wildly; the vessel shook like a dog with the ague. More leaking steam lines clouded the decks in vapor. From below came a cry of alarm as the Chinese retreated from a rush of muddy water over the port gunwales. But Rosie settled down again and her paddles dug into the Yellowstone. Slowly her bow came around; she headed upstream, paddles making a *chung chung chung* sound.

Alec wiped his brow with a sleeve. "Not a very stylish way to do it," he muttered, "but it saves time."

In the lifting fog the broad reaches of the river lay before them, a moiling flood laced with whirlpools and snags. Cottonwoods that had once flourished along its banks stood like drowned sentinels. From behind, a wan sun lit the river. Soon it would rain again. Gamble watched with glazed eyes as a huge tree trunk, root end dragging on the bottom, swept toward them. Alec hauled at the wheel. There was a scraping noise; *Rose of Dundee* winced, yawed, then settled in her marks again.

Gamble yelled above the rush of water, the cannonlike report of the high-pressure exhaust, the chunging of paddles. "That was a close one!"

Alec shrugged. "That kind doesn't worry me! It's the ones you don't see that give you fits!"

Behind them Wicket's Branch disappeared in the greenery. A vagrant shaft of sun lit Horace Tobin's big house on the hill. Below, Springer's Landing was still wrapped in river mists. No one had yet noticed their flight.

"You got any cash?" Alec asked Gamble.

The lieutenant relaxed his grip on the stanchion and looked in a wallet. "A few dollars, that's all."

"We'll have to beg, borrow, or steal cordwood. When we get up to Frenchy's place I'll see if my credit's any good, though Villard is one tightfisted breed."

They jumped when something shattered one of the side windows, spanged against a stay, screamed off upriver. Alec withdrew behind a slab of boiler plate, reaching out a long arm to hold the wheel steady.

"What in hell was that?" Gamble demanded.

With his free hand Alec put the brass spyglass to his eye.

"Over there!" Gamble gestured with the barrel of his carbine. "On that sandy point! Looks like a man on a mule!"

Focusing, Alec stared. As he did so there was a puff of smoke from the distant rifleman; another bullet caromed off the boiler plate. He shrank back, then peered shoreward again through the broken window.

"I'll be damned!" he muttered.

Gamble, moustaches twitching like an annoyed cat, propped the carbine on the sill of the broken window. "Two hundred yards, say—" He adjusted the sight with expert fingers. "No wind. Oh, maybe five miles an hour—"

Alec pushed the carbine back. "That's Woolly Willie Yates!"

"I don't care who the hell it is! When someone shoots at me, it's war!"

Alec yelled into the speaking tube. "Hugh, come up here! At once—do you hear me?"

Now the rider had spurred the mule up to its shoulders in

the swirling current and was drawing another bead. Alec ducked when he saw the white puff of smoke; the bullet glanced off the stack with a metallic clang. When his uncle stuck a whiskered face into the pilothouse, Alec was angrily brushing shards of glass from his blue uniform.

"Do you know why Woolly Willie is shooting at us?"

Hugh looked uncomfortable. He shaded his eyes with a hand. "That's him, all right!"

"I know that's him!" Alec snapped. "But why is he shooting at us? What's he mad about?"

Woolly Willie shot again. This time the bullet splashed astern.

"Well?"

Hugh hung his head. "I meant it all for the good, nephew. Swith, I wouldn't want you to think your old uncle—your own father's best-loved brother—was dishonest!"

Alec's dark brows drew together.

"You know that gold ring of mine, the one with the Munro family seal on it?" Hugh asked.

"Of course I know that ring! Father gave it to you when he died!"

Hugh took the ring from his pocket, held it out. "One day the devil came on me. I soldered this tiny mirror to the underside so I could see the cards as I dealt them out. Unfortunately, a stray bit of light from the lamp over the table caught the mirror at the wrong time. Woolly Willie remarked on it, and before I knew what was happening he chased me out of the Paradise Saloon and into the hills. I evaded him for the rest of the night, having often laid about in the bushes while doing a bit of poaching at the big McTavish place on Loch Tay—"

Seeing Alec's stern visage, he realized he was digressing. "Anyway, I gave him the slip, and near daybreak I made my way down here."

Alec turned the wheel. As *Rose of Dundee* skirted a foam-riffled bar the hostile rider faded from view.

"You cheating old scut! Willie will cut out your giblets with that big Green River knife he carries, and it will serve you right!"

Hugh grinned. "Foosh! He's slow and awkward! I can dodge round him any day!"

"Then," Alec said coldly, "show me how nimble you can be! Hurry down that ladder now and give me five more revolutions!" To Gamble he sighed, "The black sheep of the family! Otherwise the Munros have always been God-fearing Presbyterians!"

On they chuffed, the river grown dark and gray as the sun gave up the struggle, sinking beneath leaden clouds. Rosie fought the current like a champion though at times it seemed they were only holding their own. Alec pulled the wheel this way and that and the paddle-wheeler responded only sluggishly. "Not enough steerageway!" he muttered. "Uncle, give me another five revolutions!"

A huge tree bole, branches outspread, swept toward them. Alec swore, tugged at the wheel. Rosie slewed sidewise; the current caught her and turned her slowly, inexorably, around. The menacing tree swept by and was now on their bow as they found themselves pointing downstream, turned end for end, paddles flailing the waters.

"Full astern!" Alec shouted, putting the wheel hard over.

A wail came from the Chinese deckhands at the approach of disaster. The paddle wheel slowed, stopped, began to turn backward, holding them for a moment against the flood. Alec saw a backwater near shore, and quickly let the wheel pay out. Rosie yawed, shuddered, and drifted into the backwater, so near shore that heavy boughs of cottonwood brushed the red-hot stacks. Leaves fell to the deck sere and lifeless, smoldering.

"Full ahead!" Alec shouted into the speaking tube.

Slowly Rosie turned in the shallow eddy. The paddle wheel caught a low-hanging bough and chewed it up in a deluge of foliage and splintered limbs. *Rose of Dundee* pulled painfully away from shore, paddle wheel bristling with torn cottonwood saplings.

"That's better!" Alec breathed. "Well done, old girl!"

Beside him Gamble swallowed hard, fanned himself with the crumpled Kossuth hat.

Alec looked at him. "You sick?"

Gamble swallowed again, wet his lips. The weathered cheeks had taken on a faint greenish cast.

"Need something to settle your stomach," Alec advised. "There isn't much to eat aboard, but sometimes the paddle wheel shucks catfish right up out of the water and throws them on the afterdeck. Soon as one comes aboard I'll have Sam Fat fry you up a mess. Nothing better than catfish fried in hot bacon fat!" But the lieutenant was gone, fleeing down the ladder and to the rail.

"Go to the after cabin and lie down in my bunk!" Alec called after him. "You'll feel better in a day or two!"

According to the pilothouse clock it was nearing noon. Squalls of rain pockmarked the water, and the river was hard to read. A metallic glare from hidden sun stung Alec's eyes. He had had no sleep for thirty-six hours or more, and felt it. On a broad reach he shouted for Sam Fat, who was a fair pilot except in an emergency, and turned over the wheel. He himself sat on a stool, back braced against a bulkhead, grateful for a chance to close his eyes. Without knowing, he must have drifted off to sleep.

"Cats," someone in his dream remarked.

Cats? he wondered.

"Where come from damned cats?" the dream voice insisted.

What cats?

"Damn lot of cats!" the voice protested.

Alec forced open his eyes. The pilothouse was awash in cats —calico, piebald, black, white, orange, tortoiseshell. They walked, purring, across the chart table, leaving muddy paw prints. They nosed into lockers, stalked daintily about in the broken glass on deck, meowed. From below decks came Oriental shouts of alarm.

"Get away!" Sam Fat protested, trying to steer with one

hand and brush cats from the chart table with the other. He let go of the wheel for a moment and it spun like a Catherine wheel on the Fourth of July. Inadvertently Sam stepped on a tail and the cry of anguish unnerved him.

"Cap!" he cried. "Help!"

Rousing, Alec grabbed the wheel, taking a sharp rap across the knuckles from flying spokes. Coaxing Rosie back into her marks, he booted a cat through the broken window. Cursing, he ducked as an agile and affectionate tabby jumped from atop a locker and tried to perch on his shoulder, digging claws into his jacket.

"What the hell's going on here?" he cried.

Lieutenant Rollo Gamble stumbled into the cabin, holding the doorjamb for support.

"Sorry!" he apologized. "One of the crates fell to the deck and sprung open. The cats got out."

Alec turned the wheel over to Sam Fat and sank back on his stool as Gamble gathered up cats. He passed a shaking hand before his eyes. "Cats?"

"Cats," Gamble confirmed. "Among other items of cargo, we've got several crates of cats from St. Louis. The Army has got to have cats. Rats eat up government grain faster than cavalry mounts do! Cats are a valuable item at Fort Mahone."

Alec shook his aching head as if he had received a blow on the skull.

"The Chinese are gathering them up and putting them back," Gamble said soothingly. "I'll get a broom and sweep the rest of them out of the pilothouse, Captain."

Alec stared with fatigue-reddened eyes. "You needn't be formal," he said wearily. "Just call me Alec, and I'll call you Rollo. Right? Because I have an idea you and I are going to go through some remarkable experiences before we tie up at Fort Mahone."

That afternoon, after a scanty meal of stale soda crackers and coffee, Alec managed a little sleep while Sam Fat again relieved him at the wheel. Finally the Chinaman woke him.

"Cap," he asked in perplexity, "where go?"

The main course of the river had completely disappeared; all landmarks failed. The torrent was pocked with the riffles of dangerous towheads—submerged islands. In normal times Alec knew them all: Fish Head, Blazer, White Horse, Crozier's, La Boeuf's. Now he shook his head in puzzlement.

"I'll take the wheel," he decided.

River signs having failed, he scanned the chalky bluffs. That must be Rainy Butte, the towering flat-topped one. Quickly he consulted his charts and his heart sank. Only eighteen miles made good so far?

The speaking tube rasped. "Alec?"

"Yes."

"All we've got left below decks is half a cord of spongy cottonwood. How far to Frenchy's place?"

Alec looked again at the chart. "Two miles or so, nearly as I can judge."

Uncle Hugh sounded pessimistic. "Alec, I don't know!"

"Do the best you can!"

On the wide bend they now approached he must stay close inshore, where the current was slower; fuel economy was paramount. Alec knew Rosie's appetites better than his own—steam pressure, boiler-water level, paddle-dips per minute to give the highest efficiency, the most miles per cord of wood. "Throttle her down!" he yelled into the brass tube. "Give me about ten revolutions, uncle!"

Rollo Gamble, having finished the roundup of the cats, joined him. "They're putting the last stick of wood into the firebox," he reported. He glanced at the ax in its clips above the pilothouse door. "Maybe we'd better be chopping up something."

"What?" Alec demanded.

"You travel pretty bare, that's sure." Gamble scanned the hurricane deck. "Maybe that railing up front would help. And those big poles sticking up in the air—there's a lot of wood in them."

Alec recoiled at the thought of cutting into Rosie. "If you're so damned ready to throw something into the firebox," he snapped, "go get some of those boxes and barrels on the main deck and stuff them in!"

Gamble was indignant. "I'm accountable for every last item! Financially accountable! Besides, they're all needed at Fort Mahone!"

Alec squinted into the late-afternoon sun emerging from a rack of clouds. Frenchy's place had to be coming up soon. His gaze settled on a lightning-blasted pine tree, trunk pale and ghostly against the green of crowding cottonwoods. There was a tree like that just below Frenchy's.

"Alec?"

"Yes."

Hugh's voice was sepulchral. "Steam pressure's dropping."

"How much have you got?"

"Hundred and twenty-five pounds."

Alec's hands were sweaty on the wheel. If they lost headway Rosie would slide backward again, out of control. She would end her days by breaking her back on one of the murderous towheads.

"I'll settle for five revolutions!" he muttered.

Like a snail Rosie crept forward, barely making steerage-way, answering uncertainly to the wheel. Alec talked to her, coaxing her as if she were a woman, wishing her forward as they crept around a sandy bar from which birds flew in alarm.

"Come on, girl! You can do it! Remember the old story—Robert the Bruce and the spider?" He himself did not remember the details of the story, but in boyhood it had had something to do with the Bruce's stubborn persistence in the face of defeat by the hated Sassenachs—the English.

"Gauge is dropping!" Uncle Hugh announced. "Less than a hundred pounds now!"

"Cut the boiler feedwater!" Alec ordered. Where was Frenchy Villard's woodyard?

"Good losh!" Hugh protested. "Do you want to blow us out of the water?"

"I know it's dangerous! And I'm dangerous, too, when the crew doesn't obey captain's orders!"

In the murky shade of the cottonwoods along the shore it was hard to tell whether they were moving or not, except for the slow passage of trees along the starboard gunwales.

Rollo Gamble sniffed. "I smell smoke!"

"So do I," Alec agreed. It could hardly be their own; Rosie's stacks carried her smoke high and away behind. "It's near suppertime. Frenchy's probably frying meat and making coffee for supper."

"Then we're getting close, aren't we?"

Uncle Hugh's voice quavered from the speaking tube. "Nephew, pressure's going way up now! Near two hundred pounds! I don't know how much longer that old boiler will take the strain!"

"Hang on!" Alec shouted back. "We're almost there!"

Rosie's paddle-dips picked up, accelerated by the mounting steam pressure. In one last desperate surge she rounded the bar, nosed toward shore again.

"That's a hell of a lot of smoke for a cooking fire!" Rollo Gamble observed.

The shoreline was dim with smoke. Through it they could see high-piled ricks of flaming cordwood. Gamble stared at the inferno. "What—"

"The damned woodyard's burning!"

Gamble picked up his carbine. "Indians?"

Alec swung the wheel hard to starboard and yelled down the brass mouthpiece of the speaking tube. "Hugh, done with engines!" Picking up his speaking trumpet, he shouted through the broken window. "Sam Fat, take the bow line and snub her round a tree!"

Gamble blinked in surprise. "You're not going to tie up here with Sioux around!"

"Got to! We can't go anyplace without wood!"

"But they may still be lurking about!"

Alec took the Colt's revolver from the drawer where it lay beside his father's Bible. As they hurried down the ladder and onto the main deck he cried out to his uncle.

"Hugh, stand by the cannon to repel boarders! We're going ashore!"

Chapter Three

There was no time to swing out the gangplank; Alec jumped over the side into the water. Rollo Gamble, carrying the carbine, splashed after him, muttering, "I was at Chickamauga and Malvern Hill, but I never fought any Indians yet! How do you go about it?"

Alec grabbed a handful of reeds to pull himself up the bank. Wet from his plunge, he nevertheless quailed at the wall of fire. "Follow me!" he shouted to Gamble, and hurried through the burning ricks of wood. Holding a protecting hand before his face, he looked about for Indian sign. "Frenchy's got a little cabin on that rise over there." He pointed.

Gasping for breath, choking in the acrid fumes, they staggered through the inferno. A few of the ricks were still covered with canvas. As they passed, the dirty stuff charred and burst into flame and they smelled the oily stink of kerosene.

Alec stumbled and fell. His boot, scrabbling for purchase, slid into a mound of embers. He jerked it back, foot scorched.

"Frenchy!" he called. "Where the hell are you?"

Smeared with ashes and soot and beating at sparks in their clothing, they emerged from the lanes of burning cordwood. Frenchy Villard's cabin, too, had been fired. The roof of thick-butted shakes was roaring with such intensity that the updraft caught papers, clothing, an old hat, blowing them high through a flame-edged hole in the roof.

"Frenchy!" Alec yelled.

Winded, Gamble stood beside him. "If he's inside, he's dead anyway! Let's get out of here!" He pulled a fold of his scorched coat around the magazine of the carbine. "I'm afraid the heat's going to set off a cartridge and blow a hole in my butt!"

Alec stared helplessly about. "I guess so! The old man's probably done to a crisp, with his throat cut and his head bashed in!" He took off his cap, held it briefly over his breast. "Lord, take him to you! He was a pirate with his prices for wood, but for all that he was a good man, and I don't hold that against him."

Gamble looked back at the burning woodyard. "We don't have to go through that, do we? Isn't there a way around?"

Alec peered into the scorched trees surrounding the cabin. Already the heat had charred the nearest trunks, withered the leaves so that the scene resembled autumn rather than June.

"What is it?" Gamble whispered.

"Over there! Something moved!"

Together they brought their weapons to bear on a copse of river oak, trunks grown grotesquely together. Squinting along the barrel of the Colt, Alec yelled, "Come out of there, you! We've got you in our sights!"

A wizened face under a scorched straw hat looked out from the tangle of limbs.

"You!" Alec ordered. "Come out with your hands up!"

The figure stepped hesitantly from the trees. "Alec?"

"Frenchy!"

The woodhawk ran to Alec and threw his arms about him. *"Mon dieu, je suis sauvé! Merci á dieu!"* Babbling in relief, Frenchy slipped lower and lower until he clasped Alec about the knees. "Alec, you save me, *non?* My prayers, she answer!"

"Here, here, man!" Alec protested, trying to disengage him. "Stand up, now! Are you all right?"

In heavily accented English, grizzled Frenchy told them how the Sioux had come on him in late afternoon, looking for liquor. Woodhawks generally kept a barrel of forty-rod, trading pannikins full for wood or furs. "That *diable* Bad Eye!" Frenchy shuddered. "Him with his tomato cans for cuffs! He come, him and maybe twenty of his rascals! Drink up all my whiskey, tie me up while they set fire my wood with coal oil I keep for lamp! But I get away, by damn!" He rubbed bleeding wrists. "Run into *forêt*, I! Get away, watch my damn wood burn!" He gestured toward the flaming ricks. "Now what I do, Alec?"

"Get out of here, I guess," Alec said practically. "We'll take you upriver and let you off wherever you want. It's not safe here with old Bad Eye roaming about."

Frenchy sighed, his long moustaches blowing out. *"Merde!* All them wood! Well, you right, I guess!"

Alec coughed when a gust of wind blew smoke and ashes in his face. "Of course I'll have to charge you deck passage," he said thriftily. "No cash, you understand, but I'll take some of your wood in payment."

"It's all burning!" Gamble objected.

"Not completely." Alec stuck the Colt back in his belt. "If we get the Chinamen busy, we can snake a lot of it out and dump it into the river to cool off. Anyway, we haven't got a choice. We're out of fuel—have to take what we can get."

Hurrying back to *Rose of Dundee,* they emerged from the trail to find Uncle Hugh Munro with the tiny brass bow cannon trained on them and a match to the touchhole.

"Don't shoot!" Alec called. "It's us!"

Hugh peered uncertainly at them. "I guess it is," he decided, "though you look like a nickel's worth of catmeat, all of you! Hello, Frenchy!"

Quickly Alec ordered Sam Fat to muster his Chinamen. With axes, shovels, and boathooks they went to work salvaging the fuel. Much was pithy cottonwood, already turned to ashes. But among the bull pine and river oak they found solid billets, only slightly charred. These they dragged into the river to quench the smoldering, and piled them later on deck.

"By God, if we ever make it to Fort Mahone, I deserve a Presidential Commendation!" Rollo Gamble wheezed, wiping a soot-smeared face. "When I joined the Army I never counted on anything like this!"

Laboring beside the lieutenant, Frenchy Villard got a purchase on a log and rolled it aft, saying, "Hurry up, by damn! That Bad Eye maybe come back, set fire to boat too!"

Casting off the lines, they finally moved onto the river again. On the afterdeck Frenchy Villard wept as he saw his woodyard disappear around a bend. A veil like smoke from a funeral pyre lay over the scene. Wasting a few pounds of precious steam, Alec blew the whistle as they chuffed upstream into a ladder of gold. It was good to be back on the river.

None of them had eaten for a long time. Sam Fat came up the ladder bearing a greenish chunk of salt beef. "Found in bottom of barrel," he reported. "How smell, Cap?"

The stench of spoiled meat filled the pilothouse. "Good Lord!" Gamble muttered, and moved quickly away.

"All there is!" Sam Fat shrugged. "L'il bread too, maybe. Hard like rocks, though. Even rats can't chew."

"Well," Alec said, "I hate to throw anything away. Maybe if you boil it for a long time it'll kill the corruption. Then cut it up, equal shares for each man."

At dusk he called down the speaking tube to the engine room. "Uncle? Throttle her down! We're coming up on a likely towhead with a tree sticking out of it!"

The lieutenant, peering through the growing mists, was curious. "What are you planning to do?"

"Tie up for the night." Alec spoke again into the tube. "Take her down a little more—say five revolutions." Through his speaking trumpet he hailed Sam Fat. "Stand by the bow line and throw a couple of half-hitches over that stub of tree!"

"We're stopping here—in the middle of the river?"

"Best place. Safest place, with Indians about!"

"I don't mean that. I mean—we're just going to sit here all night?"

"What the hell did you expect?"

"Why, I thought you'd just keep going! After all, it's a long way to Fort Mahone, and not much time!"

Hungry and tired, eyes red from smoke and continuous

reading of the river, Alec was annoyed. "No one runs this river at night unless they damned well have to! The bars are cluttered with the bones of vessels that tried it!"

"But—"

"But me no buts!" Alec shouted. "I'm captain of this boat, and I'll run her my way!" Sagging with fatigue, he slumped on the stool. Rosie lost way, paused, then slid backward into the current. The bow line came dripping from the water, tightened, then stopped Rosie dead. She seemed to sigh, almost gratefully, creaking and whispering.

"Done with engine!" Alec rasped into the speaking tube.

Gamble was apologetic. "I'm sorry," he murmured. "You're the C.O., right enough."

Wearily Alec stared into the dusk. A blue pallor began to permeate the river mists. *Blue. Cornflower blue. Blue eyes.* He saw them in the vapors that curled up from the river.

"It's all right, Rollo," he murmured.

My true love is a blue-eyed daisy. Well, she was lost to him now, for good. The questioning blue eyes faded away into the mists. Nora Tobin was going to marry Julius Winkle; perhaps it was best that way. A stockholder in the Missouri Packet Lines, with an elevated status as captain of the fleet flagship *Sultan,* Winkle could give her all the good things of life that Alec Munro couldn't. All Alec had was old Rosie, and a good chance of going to jail for defying a writ of attachment. Sitting on the stool, he dozed, waking only when Sam Fat entered, bearing a tin plate with a fist-sized chunk of boiled beef and some bread.

"Still stink," Sam Fat reported.

Repelled, Alec waved him away and put his head on the chart table. He slept, dreaming fitfully.

In predawn darkness Uncle Hugh stoked up his banked fires. At first light *Rose of Dundee* again steamed upriver. Alec blinked in the morning rays of sun. Never had he seen such a wilderness. Familiar landmarks—Coffee Island, Massasauga Bar, Squaw Landing—all were gone, swept away, disappeared under water, or greatly changed in appearance. The wide valley of the Yellowstone was slashed with unfamiliar channels, strange bars, roaring chutes where once had been quiet stretches. Feeling almost in a foreign land, he abandoned his charts and no longer consulted the compass, steering Rosie as best he could by the look of the water. In spite of the morning chill, sweat broke out on his forehead as Rosie slipped over bars, grinding sandily, while floating trees clawed at them and debris ground along the hull.

As they lost steerageway in a maelstrom and finally swirled out, Uncle Hugh Munro's voice growled over the speaking tube. "Swith, you spilled my coffee, the last there was! What kind of course is that you're steering, boyo? It would give an eel the shakes!"

Rollo Gamble, standing at Alec's side, braced himself as Rosie heeled to starboard and then slewed back.

"Seasick, are you?" Alec gibed.

"Not seasick—hungry! God, I could eat a horse—saddle, shoes, and all!"

Alec spun the wheel quickly. A section of planked walkway, probably torn from some upstream landing, slid under Rosie's bows and thundered along her hull, emerging into the paddles with a tremendous clatter. "Damn!" he muttered. "Here, Gamble! Hold her steady!"

"What the hell do I know about steering boats?"

"You'll learn!" Alec ran to the boiler deck aft of the pilothouse and looked down. "Took off one blade and split another," he reported. "Could have been worse, though!"

Later in the day the weather became unsettled. Sun floated in and out of scudding clouds, dappling the river with dark and light. Then came quick gusts of rain and a wind that blew steadily against Rosie's bows.

"Damned ugly weather!" Gamble muttered, pulling his scorched coat tighter.

"Just like Scotland!" Alec said cheerily.

Once a quick drumbeat rattled against the boiler-iron armor of the pilothouse and clattered on the tin roof. The decks were suddenly white with hail, which melted when the sun again drifted into view.

Frenchy Villard clambered up the ladder, excited. *"Les voilá!"* He pointed to a clump of half-drowned scrub trees on a remnant of land being rapidly swept away by the current. *"Les buffles!"*

Gamble frowned. "Beefles? What the hell are beefles?"

"Buffalo," Alec explained.

"Oui!" Frenchy confirmed. *"Les buffles!* Meat—ah, good meat!" He rubbed his lean belly, smacked his lips.

Gamble borrowed Alec's spyglass. "That's right! A whole herd of steaks and chops!"

Alec shouted down the speaking tube. "Uncle, I'm heaving alongside an island! Throttle her down a few revolutions!" He yelled over the side. "Come up here quick, Sam Fat, and take her!"

Gamble, eager, rested the carbine on the window ledge and sighted. Alec quickly pushed the barrel aside. "You army people always want to be shooting things! If you hit one, it'd just fall over and be swept away!" Hurrying down the ladder, he picked up a coil of rope, fashioning one end into a noose. "Bring her close as you can, Sam Fat!" He ran past the boiler to the bows, swinging his improvised noose. Frenchy, understanding, trotted after him joyfully, muttering, *"Viande!* Meat!"

As *Rose of Dundee* nudged into the sand surrounding the drowning island, Alec swung his lariat. Several of the animals, frightened by the popping of the high-pressure exhaust, plunged into the water. Only one remained, a half-grown animal, pawing the loosening soil and bawling. "Damn!" Alec muttered. "Missed!" Casting the rope again, he caught the animal in a loop that snagged an ear, slipped down around the neck. Panicky, the beast lunged into the river and pulled Alec into the water. Hanging on to his lariat with one hand, paddling with the other, his flailing grasp caught one of Rosie's rope fender-guards.

"Frenchy!" he yelled. "Help me!"

Sprawled flat on the deck, the woodhawk grabbed Alec by the collar. The garment tore, but a few stitches held. The Chinamen came then, chattering, to drag Alec onto the deck, wet and bedraggled, but still holding the rope.

"Pull!" he wheezed. "Pull! Get him alongside before the line breaks!"

By combined effort they hauled the animal over the gunwales and dragged him, bawling and scuffling, onto the deck. Frenchy Villard snatched out his knife and cut the animal's throat. Almost before it stopped twitching the woodhawk sliced through the hairy hide from nose to tail, peeling off the pelt in one piece. "Wagh!" he exulted. *"Boudins!* Fresh liver!" He wiped a bloody hand across his face. "Nothing like meat, eh?" A good Catholic, he raised his bearded face heavenward. *"Merci, Seigneur!"*

They ate steaks and chops, roasted on a shovel held in the firebox, till they could eat no more. The cats set up a piteous wailing, pacing their cages like small tigers till scraps and offal were brought to them. Alec, hands greasy from the feast, took over the wheel again as they loosed the bow line.

"How many miles you expect we made good today?" Rollo Gamble asked, sucking marrow from a leg bone.

"Twenty miles—maybe less. The way the river twists and turns now it's hard to tell." Dusk had fallen and Alec was beginning to worry. Nowhere could he see suitable mooring for his vessel. "I guess this time we're going to have to run in to shore and tie her up."

"What about old Bad Eye or whatever his name is?"

"Got to risk it! We'll keep a deck guard during the night, and push off if they try to board. The red bastards can smell liquor ten miles away."

"Liquor? You mean you've got liquor aboard?"

Alec pointed to the line of oaken kegs lashed along the rail of the boiler deck. "Uncle Hugh's *usquebaugh*. Whisky. At least, his approximation to scotch whisky!"

"All that?" The lieutenant started to count. "One, two, three—"

"He's run his still night and day since we were served with Horace Tobin's writ. Said he was going to set up a saloon on Rosie and pay off the judgment against us."

When they brushed the tree-lined bank, Sam Fat's boys tied up Rosie for the night. "Done with engine!" Alec shouted down the speaking tube. He was grateful when Rosie's thunderous exhaust hiccuped, sighed, then settled into silence.

"I'll take the first watch," Gamble said quickly. "You're worn out, old man. The weight of command, eh? They talk a lot about that in the Army."

Carrying a plate of roasted hump-meat, Alec clambered wearily down the ladder and sank onto a bale of government-issue blankets, coarse wool prickled with burrs. Surfeited, he finally laid the plate on an ammunition box. In the flickering yellow light of the deck lamp he read CARTRIDGES, SPENCER, .56–.56, QUANTITY 500, PROPERTY U. S. GOVERNMENT. SHIP TO FORT MAHONE, I. T. During the war he had once been issued a Spencer, then only just coming into use. It was a good gun, though he didn't remember ever having hit anything with it; he was a bad shot, or perhaps it was only because he didn't want to hurt people—even rebs, or whatever they called the Southern people. Sassenachs, now—Englishmen—that was another matter. Some day Scotland would be free, and Alec and his renegade uncle would go back to Loch Tay.

Except for the sucking and the curling of the water the night was quiet. Was the river perhaps dropping a little from flood crest? A crescent moon, like a scallop of cheese, peeked from the clouds. Among the trees a gray form flitted, and he heard the cry of the owl. On deck lay the opium-drugged Chinese, cradled among boxes and sacks and kegs, dreaming of the celestial kingdom. Folding hands behind his head, Alec bemusedly observed the strange behavior of the tin plate of meat that he had laid on the ammunition box. It was moving, though very slowly. He blinked, narrowed his eyes, scratched an unshaven chin.

Taking the plate between thumb and forefinger, he stayed its progress. It tugged back at him. Wondering if fatigue had addled his brains, he stared as slender fingers drew the plate toward a cavern among the high-piled freight.

"Stop that!" he commanded.

The plate stopped.

"What the hell's going on?"

The fingers quickly disappeared.

"Who's in there?" Alec demanded. "Rollo! Rollo Gamble! Come here quick! Bring a lantern!"

Reaching into the hole, Alec caught a slim wrist. Gamble, alarmed, hovered above him, lantern in one hand and carbine at the ready. "What is it? Boarders?"

The Chinamen woke and thronged about, chattering in singsong Cantonese. Uncle Hugh Munro, wiping his hands on a clump of greasy waste, hurried from the engine room.

"I don't know what it is—yet!" Alec pulled hard. "Good Lord, man—don't stand there gaping. Carry away some of these boxes and let's see what kind of a fish I've caught!"

He jerked hard, and a figure shrouded in a dirty tarpaulin tumbled from the recess and onto the deck. Gamble leveled the carbine, snatched away the canvas. "Put your hands up, you!"

The crouching figure stood, proud and defiant, a delicate hand sweeping away the taffy ringlets now in disarray.

"Nora!" Alec's voice tended sometimes to squeak when he was in the grip of strong emotion. "Nora Tobin! What—whatever are you doing here?"

"Well!" she said icily. "I must say—this is a very violent way to greet a lady!"

Rollo Gamble dropped the carbine and extended a hand to help Nora from the folds of canvas. "Miss Tobin! This is indeed a surprise!" Sam Fat, hands tucked in sleeves, beamed from ear to ear and bobbed like a mechanical toy. Uncle Hugh, who had always got along with Nora better than Alec had, helped her by the elbow.. Alec began to feel stirrings of panic. Something had gone dreadfully wrong.

"What is the meaning of this?" he demanded.

She tossed her head. "Must I really stand here before all these people and conduct my business in public?"

Gamble rolled spiked moustaches between thumb and forefinger. "Yes, indeed, Alec," he agreed. "It's hardly proper, now, is it?" Uncle Hugh chimed in. "Alec, don't you see the poor lass is a bit travel-worn?"

The clinging white gown Alec remembered from Nora's engagement party was spattered with mud and she had lost a slipper. A rent in the hem of the sequined gown showed a disturbing expanse of ankle.

"Conduct your business?" Alec croaked. "Whatever business can you have with me, girl?" Somehow it made him uncomfortable to see Rollo Gamble brazenly eyeing Nora's ankle. "All right," he relented. "Come along to the after cabin with me and we'll see what this is all about." Over his shoulder he called with heavy emphasis to Gamble. "Keep your eyes on the *shoreline,* Lieutenant! That's what's important!"

In his small cabin he lit a lamp and motioned her to his single chair, a cane-bottomed relic with the seat half out. He was ashamed of the disorder; dirty clothes, dried mud on the deck, smelly boots, the odors of a man living a close and untidy existence. Still and all, he hadn't asked her to come aboard.

"Now please explain yourself!"

Some of the immodest red stuff on her lips had rubbed off, and she looked pale. She swayed, put a hand to her forehead.

"Are you sick?" Ladies' indispositions made him uneasy.

"No—just hungry. When I smelled that meat I couldn't resist." She looked at him with a shade of the old defiance. "If it hadn't been for that you'd never have caught me!"

Ashamed of his severity, he found a few overlooked slices of meat and a chunk of bread. Cutting off the dirty end of the loaf, he brought her the food. "I'm sorry," he apologized, "but this is all there is."

She ate wolfishly, gobbling down the meat and sopping the greasy juices with the bread. Miss Waddell, he thought with satisfaction, would have been shocked at her student's manners. When she took a deep breath and sat back in the chair, dabbing the clefted chin with a lacy handkerchief, he resumed his questioning.

"Pray tell me what you're doing on my boat!"

A small belch escaped her. In embarrassment she spread a hand across her bosom. "Oh, my!"

"That's all right."

"It's just—just that I haven't eaten for two days." She swallowed; for a moment the breath caught in her throat, like a small child after crying. "At the house I didn't eat much on account of being so upset, and I've been on Rosie for what seems like an eternity."

He remained insistent. "Why did you come here?"

"I want to go upriver to see my Aunt Belle Goggins. She lives at Turkey Flats, just below Fort Mahone. I've got money, Alec—a little, anyway. I can pay fare like any other passenger."

"But you're engaged to Julius Winkle!"

"It's none of your business who—I mean whom I'm engaged to, Alec Munro! Do you demand references from all your passengers?"

Stung, he pointed out a discrepancy. "My passengers usually pay their passage in advance, come aboard in a proper way, and stroll about the deck instead of hiding in the cargo! Whatever mischief are you planning, Nora Tobin?"

Her chin trembled, but she remained defiant. "What I plan is my own business, and does not concern you, Alec Munro!"

He ran a hand through his hair. "But don't you see I can't afford to get into more trouble with your pa? Damn it all, I'm in hot water already!" His eyes narrowed. "Did you run away from home or something? And how did you know I was taking Rosie up to Fort Mahone?"

She smiled in a way he thought patronizing. "Bessie was on the veranda that night you and Lieutenant Gamble left. She overheard you talking to Lieutenant Gamble—he *is* a charming man—about breaking Sheriff Bagley's chain and leaving in spite of father's lien on your boat. She came and told me directly. So she helped me pack my bag and here I am!"

"Then why were you hiding?"

"Because," she said, yawning and speaking in a slow and distinct manner, as to a child, "if you knew I was aboard you'd put me off, wouldn't you? Now you can't do that—I mean, with Indians all around and wild animals in the forest."

Exasperated, he gnawed a knuckle. Nora was right, of course; for better or worse, he was stuck with her.

"So," she said airily, "if you'll just go up to the front of your boat—"

"Forward!"

"I beg your pardon?"

"You go forward," he muttered. "There's no damned *front* on a boat." In the old days, he remembered, she used to know things like that. Miss Waddell's school had ruined her.

"Anyway, up there in a kind of little nest I made among the boxes and barrels and things you'll find my valise, Alec. I must get out of these raggedy things and put on something fresh." Daintily she picked up the hem of the bedraggled gown, examined the tear. "Caught my heel in it, I suppose, while I was running down the hill. But Aunt Belle is such a good seamstress! I'm sure she can fix it like new."

Defeated, he rose. "I'll get your bag. Uh—this cabin is a bit untidy, I guess. I'll have one of Sam Fat's Chinamen clean it up."

"Thank you," Nora said sweetly. "I knew I could count on you, Alec!"

Count on me, he thought angrily. Nora had always taken him for granted, the way he saw it—maneuvered him, schemed with her woman's wiles. Good, steady old Alec! Faugh!

Searching in the cargo for her bag, he had just found the

bulky valise with its squared brass corners when he heard Rollo Gamble challenge someone on shore. He straightened just in time to see Sheriff Ben Bagley jump across the narrow gap between *Rose of Dundee* and the bank. Ben's shotgun had the drop on Gamble.

"Hold steady, everyone!" the sheriff warned. "Don't nobody move!"

Alec, holding the valise, gaped at Ben and the mud-spattered buckboard and team on the bank. "Where the hell did *you* come from, Ben?" Two unexpected visitors in one night was too many.

With the light of triumph in his eyes, the old man sidled forward. Spattered with mud, he looked like an Egyptian mummy recently exhumed. "It was a long hard trip with the roads the way they are," he said. "I got bogged down a lot, and never thought I'd catch up with you, but I did! Now, Goddamnit, Alec, I got to place you under arrest for removing lawfully sequestered property from the place where it was attached, or maybe the words goes the other way round—I don't recollect and I ain't got my law book with me! And besides all that— what in hell have you done with Horace Tobin's daughter— Miss Nora?"

Chapter Four

Alec stared in disbelief. "How did you ever get here?"

The sheriff stepped forward warily. "By riding hard on the old Hatcher trail and endangering an old man's health—which is me—to catch a lawbreaker." His clothing was torn, one boot had lost a heel, and he breathed heavily. "Alec, ding it, I warned you! Why did you do it, son?" From the corner of his eye Bagley detected a movement by Rollo Gamble. "You, mister! Don't move or I'll wool lightning out of you!"

Gamble stared at the bearded face. "I'm not moving," he reported, and did not.

Alec stepped forward hesitantly, carrying the heavy valise. "Ben, this is a very complicated business! It's hard to discuss matters with you holding that blunderbuss! Put it away, now, so we can sit down and talk this over reasonable!"

In the light of the deck lamps they ringed Ben Bagley, keeping a respectful distance; Uncle Hugh, Sam Fat and the Chinese, Frenchy Villard, a cautious Rollo Gamble. "That's right, Ben," Uncle Hugh urged. "This ain't what it appears to the eye!" Drawn by the hubbub, Nora Tobin appeared at the doorway of her cabin, one hand holding together an unlaced bodice.

"Uncle Ben!" she cried. Although no blood relation, Ben Bagley had always been Uncle Ben to most of the children of Springer's Landing. "What are you doing here?"

"Miss Nora!" the old man cried in relief. "Lordy, am I glad to see you! The rascals ain't harmed you, have they? Because if they have—"

Alec, knowing the sheriff's unwavering dedication to the

manhunt, moved to Ben Bagley's flank while he was occupied with Nora. Seizing his chance, he swung the brass-cornered valise with force and intent. The shotgun flew from the sheriff's hands and blew a hole in the hurricane deck. Quickly Rollo Gamble knelt and rummaged in the pockets of the recumbent figure, muttering, "There's probably a set of manacles in here someplace!" Nora Tobin, eyes wide and a hand pressed to her mouth, stared accusingly at Alec.

"You've killed him!"

Alec bent over the sheriff, listened. "I didn't either! Just stunned him a little, that's all!"

Gamble found Ben's manacles and snapped them on the sheriff's wrists. Nora, Bagley's grizzled head cradled in her arms, cried, "Look! He's coming around! Oh, you poor dear— what have they done to you?"

The sheriff opened his eyes, blinked. "Somebody hit me," he decided.

Alec tried to find a way to get the incriminating valise out of sight. It was heavy, and for a moment he feared injury to Ben Bagley's skull. "It was me," he admitted sheepishly. "I did it, Ben. I'm sorry, but—"

"There was no need!" Nora said.

"Nora, you don't understand all that's at stake here!" He motioned to one of the Chinamen to take Nora's valise. "Go to your cabin now, and rest! This has been a hard day for all of us. I—I'll explain later."

"But I want to take care of Uncle Ben!"

He put on the mien of the captain of a vessel. "Damn it, Nora, go to your cabin! Rollo and I will take care of Ben!"

Sullenly she followed the Chinaman. Retreating, she turned toward him a look of such haughtiness that he almost quailed. "You're a brute, Alec Munro!" she snapped, and slammed the door.

Gamble's eyes shone. "By Harry!" he said. "Miss Tobin is beautiful when she's provoked!"

"I don't know about that, but a woman aboard a boat is

nothing but trouble. Why did she have to turn up on *my* vessel?"

With Gamble helping, Ben Bagley got shakily to his feet. Rubbing the goose egg on his bald pate, he glared at Alec. "Now you done it! On top of everything else, resisting a peace officer in the lawful carrying-out of his duties!"

Alec picked up the shotgun, broke it open, removed the cartridges. "Ben, I'm sorry. You and I are old friends!"

"Hell of an old friend *you* are—beat me over the head and take away my weapon whilst I'm making an arrest!"

"No harm will come to you, Ben," Alec apologized.

Gamble frowned. "What will we do with him, then?"

"I'll put him in Uncle Hugh's cabin and chain him to a steam pipe. It's smelly, but it's got a stout door and no windows." He put a hand on the sheriff's shoulder. "Ben, nobody's forgot the time you went after the McAllister twins when they blew the safe in the bank and went riding off to Bismarck with ten thousand dollars of Missouri Packet Lines money. You never give up, Ben, so I've got to take that into account. Till I get Lieutenant Gamble's supplies to Fort Mahone I've got to keep you tied up." He turned to Gamble. "Take him forward and secure him, like I said. Uncle Hugh's got some chain and a padlock."

When Gamble returned, Alec had Sam Fat and the Chinese hard at work. The Chinamen had taken the wheels off Bagley's buckboard and were hoisting it aboard. The sheriff's rust-colored mare was tied on the afterdeck, munching oats from a feed bag. Alec watched a coolie roll an ironbound wheel aboard and called, "Tie the wheels to that stanchion there!"

"What in hell are you doing?" the lieutenant asked. "It'll be light soon. We ought to be getting up steam! Fort Mahone, remember—no later than the twelfth of June!" Exasperated, he watched the mare deposit a pile of fresh manure on the deck. "Why didn't you just roll that old buggy into the river and turn the mare loose? We're in a hurry!"

"Because," Alec explained, "that old buggy is a genuine

Jagger, and Ben's fond of it. He polishes it up every Sunday to take the Widow McKeever to church. That roan mare is Pepperpot. Half the kids in Springer's Landing learned to ride on Pepperpot's grandfather, old Missouri Rambler. I can't let anything happen to Pepperpot. Ben would never forgive me—or Nora, either."

Rosie's whistle sounded, a wavering and uncertain sound with little steam behind it.

Gamble shook his head. "I don't believe this! What the hell is going on here—a military operation or a family reunion?"

Alec listened to a louder blast of the whistle. "There!" he said with satisfaction. "We've got a head of steam."

Gamble sighed. "Once I had a promising career—rising young attorney in Boston, fine record in the War, meritorious service in the Judge Advocate General's office. Now look at me! Criminal conspiracy to steal a steamboat, accessory to the kidnapping of a young female, resisting arrest, and assaulting a peace officer! But all *you* can talk about is a damned buggy and some horse's grandfather! It's enough to make a man cry!"

Alec snorted. "Hell, you're *Army,* Rollo! Out here in the Territory the Army can get away with anything it wants to! What you did, you did under *orders,* and that's a different thing! No, Rollo—you're clean as drifted snow compared to me. I'm in this up to my ears and sinking fast. I'm not Army. I'm not anything but a raggedy river pilot that won't have any three-star general speaking up for him. So shut up, my beauty, and play dumb! You're getting on my nerves!"

The river was dropping. As they chuffed away from the bank in the clear light of dawn Alec scanned the reaches of the Yellowstone. The massive June rise had passed and now rolled downriver. The sky was blue and cloudless. From heavily forested banks the greenery sent up tendrils of sun-warmed vapor. Birds called, northbound geese honked overhead, deer came to the water's edge to drink, but skittered away at the cannonading of Rosie's exhaust.

Rollo Gamble, bent over the chart table with a pair of dividers, made an entry in his notebook and grimaced at the noise. "Isn't there any way to quiet down that damned engine? It's splitting my skull wide open!"

"That's how a high-pressure engine operates!"

Red-eyed, and with a heavy stubble on his chin, the lieutenant swore. "I've heard St. Louis boats that were a hell of a lot quieter!"

"Low-pressure boats!" Alec was scornful. "Baby carriages, for timid people and fair-weather masters!"

"What's wrong with low pressure, then?"

"Well, they're safer—not so apt to blow passengers and crew sky high. But they don't have the power and maneuverability *Rose of Dundee*'s got. No—on a wildcat river like the Yellowstone, give me two hundred pounds of steam anytime!"

Gamble gestured with the dividers. "We've still got over three hundred miles to Fort Mahone. However are we going to make it in time?"

"Pray! And hope the river don't go too low."

"Too low? With all that water we had?"

"Sometimes, after a big rise, the Yellowstone drops way low. Kind of like a pendulum, you might say. It'll swing back and forth for a few days till it finds its proper summer level again."

Gamble groaned.

"Sometimes," Alec said, "I've seen her go so low in June it was like having old Rosie on dry land and sending a boy ahead with a sprinkling can to dampen the grass. But for now it's a sunny day, God's in His heaven and morning's new born or whatever Browning said. Go down on deck and stroll around, take the air."

"Maybe I will." Staring over the wheel, the lieutenant's eye brightened; he straightened the Kossuth hat to a rakish angle. "Why, there's Miss Nora taking her ease on that chair in the front—I mean the bows. What a delightful sight in that flowered gown and Leghorn hat!"

With all the clothes she had packed in that valise, Alec wondered how he had escaped crushing Ben Bagley's skull like an eggshell. What on earth did a woman want with all those clothes?

In midmorning he nudged Rosie into the bank long enough for Frenchy Villard to mount Pepperpot bareback and ride the mare into the underbrush, promising to meet *Rose of Dundee* upriver with deer meat. The roan pranced and caracoled at the strange rider, but Frenchy had a soothing way with animals.

"Horse, be easy! I *ami des chevals*—friend to all horse! *Tiens*—that be better!"

"Look out for Sioux!" Alec called.

Frenchy grinned, brandished the Spencer carbine Gamble had loaned him. "By damn, this gun she shoot all day—not like my old Hawken Bad Eye steal!"

Alec was still worried. Sioux did not like to get wet in the rain any more than white men did; in fair weather, then, they might be expected to expand their depredations. Still, the ship's company needed food—meat, red meat. Already the Chinese were complaining.

Resuming the wheel, he became aware of a pretty tableau forward. Lieutenant Rollo Gamble, booted foot on a spoke of the capstan, lounged at Nora's side, chatting. Alec picked up his spyglass and trained it on the pair. He was right; Gamble must have rushed to his cabin and spruced up for the encounter. The lieutenant was in fresh dress blues. In the morning sun the corps emblem on the well-brushed hat sparkled like a gem. The spiky moustache was recently waxed, and Gamble had just shaved.

"Blast him!" Alec muttered, jamming the spyglass shut. "Dallying with a female while I sweat blood up here!" Like Alec, the lieutenant had not slept for some two days and was near the ragged edge of endurance. But while Alec Munro resembled a scarecrow, Gamble was the image of the dashing cavalryman.

Uncle Hugh, having settled the engine into a powerful

fifteen revolutions, climbed the ladder and entered the pilot-house. He smelled of steam, engine oil, and sweat, but Alec detected a new element.

"Been into that devil's brew already this morning! You smell like a pub!"

Hugh wiped his mouth with a bit of cotton waste. "Aye, I have! The Elixir is a bit raw yet, but with a few more days aging it'll come prime!" He pursed his lips thoughtfully, narrowed his eyes under bushy brows. "What the hell's got into you this morning already? You're gloomy as an undertaker when no one's died!"

"Fate," Alec sighed. "There's a black dog on my back."

Glancing forward, his uncle grinned. "I see the nature of the black dog. But is that any way to speak of an officer and a gentleman in the U. S. Cavalry?"

Alec laughed, hollowly.

"Don't deny it, nephew! You're jealous, that's all."

"Me? Jealous of that flibbertigibbet with her haughty ways and heart of stone?"

Hugh stuffed the waste into a pocket of his jumper. "Ah, you're as stiff-necked as your late father! Andrew Munro was my brother, but he was just as muckle-headed as you when he was young, without the leavening of sweetness and reason I pride myself on!"

"Leave Father out of this," Alec said stiffly.

"It's God's truth! Julia Gordon, that became your mother, was high-spirited like Nora. She loved your father, but like all lassies she wanted a bit of larking about, and laughing, and playing the fool. Andrew always looked like a storm cloud, and stood on his dignity, just like you, boyo! I tell you, it was something of a miracle when he unbent once to tell her he loved her. And if 'twasn't for that, you'd never be here today, Alec Munro!"

"Save me your preaching! I'm a grown man, and know my mind!"

"You're a grown *fool*," Hugh growled, "and ought to be put

away in an institution for the addlepated! This river you may know, Rosie you may know, but you don't know females!" In sudden recollection he added, "Ben Bagley wants to have a word with you."

"What about?"

Hugh took the wheel, shrugged. "Didn't say."

In the dark confines of Hugh Munro's cabin Sheriff Ben Bagley sat on the sagging cot, wrist manacled to a steam pipe. From time to time the leaky pipe hissed vapor into the air.

"I'm dying of suffocation in here!" Ben complained, wiping his forehead with a bandanna. "What with the stink of steam, dirty clothes, and whisky!"

"I'm sorry about that," Alec apologized. "But look on it as a compliment. I daren't risk letting you go or you'd have me back in your jail!"

Ben sighed. "What in hell did you hit me with last night?"

Alec felt uncomfortable. "Well, it—it wasn't your usual kind of weapon. It was—" He hesitated. "When you came aboard like that, I just happened to have Nora Tobin's valise in my hand. She was a stowaway, you see, and we'd just found her hiding amongst the cargo."

"A stowaway? You mean she was running away?"

"I guess so. Anyway, I kind of sidled up and hit you with it."

The sheriff closed his eyes, swallowed hard. "A—a lady's valise?"

"It was all that came to hand."

"I hope this don't get around. The McAllister twins shot me in the leg. I don't mind that so much, but a valise—"

"I'll never tell," Alec promised.

"Well," Ben said, rubbing the knot on his head, "you been square with me, Alec, spite of what you done. So I'll square with you. I got to tell you you ain't home free yet, not by a long shot."

"What do you mean?"

"I mean that when Miss Nora turned up missing and

Horace found out you and Lieutenant Gamble and his cargo had went upriver on *Rose of Dundee,* he was madder 'n hell! He figured you'd carried off his little gal, so he ordered Winkle to fire up *Sultan.* Right now Horace and Captain Winkle are somewhere behind you and gaining fast."

"Not gaining on me! Not gaining on old Rosie! Even with a full deckload, Rosie'll show her heels to any boat on the Yellowstone! Anyway, Winkle's a Missouri pilot—he doesn't know this river the way I do. Surer 'n God made little apples, he'll run *Sultan* on a bar and break her back!"

"I wouldn't be too sure," Ben cautioned. "You run off with his intended, he thinks, and he's a determined man. You're young, Alec, and inclined to be rash. Don't underestimate Julius Winkle. He's smart, and mean as a badger!"

Alec rose. "Thanks for the advice, Ben, but I'm not scared of Julius Winkle."

Mournfully the sheriff rattled his chains. "Good God, you're not just going away and leave me sitting here in this place? Don't Hugh Munro ever wash his socks?"

"Every summer," Alec said, "about half-past July."

Ben sagged. "All right! I give up! Let me free of this outhouse and I give you my word I'll not harm you, or do anything to hinder—till you get to Fort Mahone, anyway, which is where I figure you're probably headed now that you've busted my official padlock and disobeyed a court order."

"Done!" Alec said quickly. "You know your word's good enough for me, Ben! I'll tell Hugh to bring the key and turn you loose. By the by, Frenchy Villard's out on your mare looking for venison. I know you're hungry—we're all hungry—but for supper we can fry up some meat."

"Thank you, son," Ben said. "I wish you hadn't broke the law, but there's no hard feelings between us, is there?"

"No, of course not."

As he was mounting the ladder again Rosie dragged, yawed, rasped sandily. Engine popping, paddles thrashing, she slowed in her ways while Uncle Hugh Munro muttered Gaelic curses. Alec hurried into the pilothouse and snatched the wheel. "And what have you done to her now?"

"Swith, it wasn't my fault!" Hugh protested. "I'm sober as a treeful of owls! It's just the river—the damned contrary river—that's to blame! Looked like Loch Tay, it did, all deep water and sunbeams! Then the spiteful old hag belches up a new bar! Wasn't anything there before!"

"Hurry aft and give me all the power you've got astern! But first, stop by your cabin and unlock Uncle Ben. He's promised me his parole."

It was a common maneuver, running the paddle wheel backward at high speed to wash away sand from the vessel's broad bottom. As the blades thrashed in reverse, gouts of muddy water poured onto *Rose of Dundee*'s afterdeck. Attracted by the clamor, Rollo Gamble came to the pilothouse.

"What's going on?"

"A wee grounding," Alec muttered. "Look out for flying catfish!"

"Flying what?"

Rosie shuddered, heeled, slid backward, then stuck again.

"Is that all you've got?" Alec yelled into the speaking tube. "Run her up a little more!"

There was a dull thud on the pilothouse roof. A mud-colored fish slithered off and fell to the main deck, twitching.

"Wheel turning backward shucks 'em up," Alec explained. "Look—the Chinamen have got it already! Fish for dinner!"

There was a hissing noise from the speaking tube; even without the aid of that device they could hear Hugh Munro cursing, and saw a cloud of steam rising aft.

"Safety valve popped!" Alec groaned.

"Isn't that dangerous?"

Alec found himself thinking of Julius Winkle and *Sultan*. Julius just might have a run of good luck to compensate for lack of piloting skill. Even now *Sultan* might be around the last bend, bearing down on them.

"Life is dangerous," he said, "but we've got to get off this bar in a hurry!"

Again the high-pressure engine roared as Uncle Hugh reset the safety valve. "Come on, old girl!" Alec urged, pushing against the wheel as if to aid Rosie in her travail. "You can do it, sweetheart!"

Finally Rosie clawed free, backed into quiet water, trembling like an exhausted racehorse. "She made it!" Alec exulted. "By God, she always does! I can trust *her!*"

Remembering Frenchy Villard, he wondered if the racket had alerted old Bad Eye and his Sioux. Rosie's laboring single-cylinder engine must have been audible ten miles distant. But in midafternoon the woodhawk hailed them from a brush-strewn bar, a fat buck across Pepperpot's withers. They picked him up and steamed on. While Ben Bagley cleaned mud and burrs from his pet, Frenchy butchered the deer.

"One fine *cheval,* your horse," he told the sheriff. "Oh, she spook a l'il when I throw that deer on her, but she settle down when I talk to her like *jolie femme*—pretty womans!"

The odor of roasting meat made them ravenous. Nora joined them, flower-sprinkled frock a strange note in the rude company. Behind his hand Rollo Gamble spoke to Alec; Sam Fat was topside at the wheel.

"Ah—don't you think we ought to do this a little more elegantly?"

"Do what more elegantly?"

Gamble cleared his throat. "Well, I mean—it's just that Miss Tobin is a lady. Surely you don't expect her to hunker down on deck like the rest of us and gnaw bones? There's an old deal table and a couple of chairs in the forward storeroom where your uncle keeps engine parts. I thought I'd just set it up in the bows, being it's such a nice day, and—"

"Do what you please," Alec said curtly. He turned to Frenchy. "See any Sioux sign? Bad Eye?"

The woodhawk had raw deer liver on a tin plate. He cut it into chunks, spearing one on the point of his knife and smacking his lips as he swallowed. *"Bon* for make love," he explained. He reached for another chunk. He scratched his head. "Bad Eye? No, I not see nothing."

The Chinamen, preferring fish, broiled the huge mud-cat. When they ran out of that they gorged themselves on venison. Ben Bagley squatted beside Uncle Hugh, holding a half-raw cutlet between his teeth, snicking off each bite with the penknife hanging from the gold chain across his vest. Uncle Hugh had drawn a pitcher of whisky and he passed it generously about.

Alec rose with a sigh, wiping greasy hands on his trousers. "I'd better go up and relieve Sam Fat."

"Any meat left," Frenchy said, belching, "I hang on rail to dry in sun. *Bien?"*

"Fine," Alec said, patting his stomach. "Fine!"

It was late afternoon, sun well down in the western sky. A scatter of cottony clouds sailed high, nether sides tinged with rose. *Red sky at night, sailor's delight?* Old rules didn't hold on the Yellowstone, though. Still, the unseasonal storms seemed to have vanished. Perhaps they could look forward to a spell of good weather. Alec felt good; back on the river again, satiated with meat, everything running smoothly. But as he mounted the ladder and entered the pilothouse he suffered a sudden attack of dyspepsia. In the bows, like a fashionable illustration from the pages of *Leslie's Illustrated Weekly,* Rollo Gamble and Nora Tobin sat at table in animated conversation. Chin propped on intertwined fingers, Nora leaned toward the lieutenant, who cut a tidbit of meat from his platter and offered it on a fork. As he did so Gamble's little finger extended outward in a fancy gesture.

"Damned fool!" Alec muttered.

At the wheel, Sam Fat turned. "What you say, Cap?"

Rays of the low-slanting sun lit Nora Tobin's high-piled hair from behind, creating an aureole of rich color. In spite of the fact that Alec knew she could be a very devil, at that moment she looked like an angel descended from the pink-tinged clouds to bless the decks of *Rose of Dundee*.

"I didn't say anything! Mind your own business, will you?"

Nora was not his, had never been, would never be. Nora was a rich girl, meant for society balls, opulent mansions, carriages grinding up gravel drives to halt beneath elegant *porte-cochères*. It took someone like Lieutenant Rollo P. Gamble, lawyer turned cavalryman, to snare her with smooth talk and fancy-Dan ways. *My true love is a blue-eyed daisy*. He sighed. He had better forget the old song.

"Go below," he snarled to Sam Fat, "and get something to eat!"

Staring into emptiness, he stood bemused at the wheel, steering mechanically. He felt sad, sad with the bone-deep melancholy of the Highlander. Thinking of a romantic suicide —maybe *that* would make Nora Tobin sorry—he stared at Bobcat Butte, just coming into view. The butte was pretty high; they could stop Rosie long enough for him to climb up and jump.

"Alec!"

In his reverie a woman's voice called.

"Yes," he murmured. "Yes—Nora."

"Alec!"

This time the voice was louder, with an edge of alarm. It was a man's voice. Alec opened his eyes, stared about. No one was in the pilothouse but himself.

"Yes!" he answered, puzzled. "Who—"

"*Alec!* Goddamnit, look!"

On the foredeck the elegant tableau had dissolved. The deal table was overturned. Nora Tobin was staring upriver, hand to her mouth. Rollo Gamble waved his arms like a madman, pointing. "Look!"

Alec's eye followed the gesture.

"Oh, my God!" he muttered.

In his brainless moonings he had not seen them. A few hundred yards ahead, making a savage line across their course, painted and feathered Sioux sat horses belly-deep in the shallows. Between them was only a narrow channel.

"Indians!" Gamble yelled. Taking Nora's arm, he pulled her after him, running to shelter under the hurricane deck.

"Of course they're Indians!" Alec muttered, gripped in indecision. "What in hell did you think they were—Hottentots?"

It would take a long time for *Rose of Dundee* to lose headway, so they could hardly turn away from the peril. Besides, there was neither time nor room to maneuver. Suddenly he decided.

"Full ahead, uncle!" he roared into the speaking tube.

As Rosie gathered speed, Alec could make out the garish armlets on the brave in the middle, the tomato cans with lids cut out and strung in unbroken array from wrist to shoulder, red labels prominent. Bad Eye himself! He and his bucks were after liquor again!

Hugh Munro's voice came shrilly from the brass bell of the speaking tube. "That's all I've got, Alec! What's happened?"

"Bad Eye!" Alec shouted. "All hands stand by to repel boarders!"

Chapter Five

Under forced draft Rosie's paddles picked up speed, churning foam. Sparks poured from her stacks, the high-pressure exhaust sounding to Alec like the cannons on the ridge at Gettysburg. Seeing the vessel steaming into the trap, the Sioux let out a shrill yell and brandished weapons. From below, on the main deck, came the *spat* of a carbine. That had to be Rollo Gamble. One of the braves toppled from his paint pony and fell into the water. The rest, undismayed, gathered their mounts and quirted them into the water until the horses swam, heads arched high and powerful quarters pumping.

An arrow broke the forward pilothouse window to lodge in the rim of the oaken wheel. As *Rose of Dundee* steamed into the water-borne horsemen the Indians parted before her like the Red Sea for the Israelites. Alec heard the roar of Ben Bagley's shotgun. He could imagine the turmoil below; red Indians clambering aboard, war hatchets raised. The whoops and savage glee he had to imagine also; the engine was making too much noise to hear anything else. But Nora! Panic gripped him. Where was Nora?

Quickly he reached for the rope bridle to hold Rosie steady in her marks. Though the river slanted sharply to starboard a quarter mile ahead, he would have to take the chance.

Kicking aside the pilothouse door he ran aft to the boiler deck and looked over, revolver in hand. On the main deck all was confusion. Frenchy Villard was down, sprawled flat. Ben Bagley, surrounded by screeching savages, swung his empty shotgun savagely; at his feet a Sioux with a broken arm crawled away. Another, hunched on his knees, held his skull in pain. On the afterdeck the sheriff's roan reared in fright, neighing.

"Ben!" Alec yelled. "Look out!"

As a brave skulked behind the sheriff, raising a ribboned hatchet, Alec shot, but succeeded only in winging the man. Howling, the Indian dropped the weapon, staring skyward to see the source of his pain.

"You there!" Alec shouted, and shot several times at another ruffian about to choke Uncle Hugh Munro. He missed, but the Sioux was distracted by the whistle of the balls past his ear. Uncle Hugh recovered enough to brain him with a spanner.

"Nora!" Alec cried. "Where are you?" He ran about the hurricane deck, searching, calling. "Nora!"

Below, Sam Fat laid about him with a cleaver. Sioux scattered like frightened crows from a grainfield. Alec could see none of the coolies. Terrified of Indians, they were probably huddled in the bilges.

"Nora!" he shrieked.

At last he found her, backed against the gunwales in the bow with Lieutenant Rollo Gamble heroically shielding her, fending off Indians with one hand while trying to reload the carbine. Nora, hair in disarray and skirt almost torn off, stood fast in lacy pantaloons and little else as she swung a mop handle.

"Hold on!" Alec shouted. "I'm coming!"

Breaking the action of the Colt and shoving in fresh cartridges, he saw that the Sioux had managed to separate the beleaguered pair. Gamble was left alone in the bows, struggling with a half dozen assailants. A Sioux brave with face painted black wrapped his arms about Nora and dragged her away.

"Nora!" Alec yelled.

He was about to vault over the rail and chance breaking a leg in the drop to the main deck, but all things considered Rollo Gamble appeared to be in more immediate peril. Knowing Nora Tobin, he guessed it would take some time for the leering brave to work a lustful will on *her*. Snatching the knife from its sheath at his belt, he ran to one of the two long oak spars. Their butt ends were secured on the main deck and they were held in a vertical position by rope stays.

"Hang on, Nora!" he muttered.

Peering down at Gamble and his opponents, he climbed unsteadily onto the rail. With a calculating eye, he put one foot against the great spar, then cut the line securing it upright. For a moment it stayed erect, surprised by freedom. Slowly and ponderously it started to fall. At the last moment Alec gave it a shove with his foot, steering it in its destructive arc. But he reached too far. Scrambling for balance, he teetered on the rail and fell.

The spar dropped also, landing like a thunderbolt among the besieging Sioux. When it hit the deck it splintered, making a report like a cannon. Some of the braves were caught beneath it; others, terrified of what seemed the wrath of tribal gods, plunged over the side. Alec, half stunned, lay flat on deck, able only to raise his head and look about.

The concussion of the falling spar had ended the battle. Someone throttled down the engine. Alec saw Sam Fat hurrying to the pilothouse just as Rosie brushed against trees on the southern shore of the river. Frenchy Villard had taken a ball through the fleshy part of his upper arm and was struggling to sit up, swearing French oaths, while Ben Bagley attempted to calm him. What drained the remaining strength from Alec's maltreated body was the sight of Nora Tobin in the embrace of Lieutenant Rollo Gamble. Rollo's arm hung limply—perhaps broken—and there was a gaping hole in the knee of his dress-blue trousers. The moustache was skewed in a nonregulation manner and one eye was puffed and swollen preparatory to turning green and purple. Nora, shameless in pantaloons, clung to Gamble—not so much in fright, Alec suspected, as in unmaidenly passion.

"Alec!" Uncle Hugh bent over him. "Good Lord, boyo, speak to me! It's your uncle!"

Alec had a splitting headache; his lungs heaved trying to recover the breath that had been knocked from him. Attempting to speak, he could manage little but a feeble croak.

"You still smell like a Goddamned brewery," he finally managed.

Hugh was indignant. "I haven't touched a drop this blessed day! What it was—one of them devils got to the boiler deck just after you jumped and bashed in the head of a whisky keg with his hatchet! It kind of got splashed all over me when I ran up there and grappled with him." He looked astern where the band of Sioux, Bad Eye leading the rout, were swimming to shore, shouting Indian maledictions and shaking their fists at *Rose of Dundee.*

"They'll be back," Uncle Hugh muttered. "They had a look at a muckle of prime scotch, and they'll be back, mark my words!" He got an arm under Alec's shoulder and started to lift him. Then he said, "It's your head, boyo! You're bleeding!" He laid Alec gently down and called. "Miss Nora! Alec's hurt!"

Alec's skull throbbed where it must have struck the oak planking of Rosie's deck. Feebly he protested. "Damn it, don't call her! Can't you see she's busy?" But he swooned, sinking into an enveloping blackness.

When he woke he was lying in his own cabin. Something smelled sour and acrid. Opening an eye, he closed it again; the flicker of the candle hurt his eyes. He fumbled at his cranium, where the pain was. Someone restrained him, saying, "Don't touch it, Alec."

"What the hell is on my head?" he grumbled.

"Just brown wrapping paper soaked in vinegar! It's good for you. My Aunt Belle always used it for Papa's headaches."

"Nora?" he asked.

"Yes, it's me."

Humiliated, he tried to struggle up. She pushed him against the pillow. "Alec Munro, now don't you be stubborn!"

Unwilling for her to see him brought low, he grudgingly opened his eyes. Around him was a blurred panorama of faces. Rollo Gamble stood in candlelight, splinted arm in a sling. Frenchy Villard squatted beside the bed, naked from his lean waist upward, a blood-soaked bandage around his arm. Ben Bagley appeared unscathed, but looked worried. Sam Fat was probably at the wheel. Uncle Hugh, Alec hoped, was tending the engine; each explosion of the exhaust made his battered skull throb.

"Glad you came to, old man," Gamble said conversationally. "You must have hit your head quite a whack."

"Someone did for your arm, too, I see," Alec murmured.

"Indian war club." Gamble shrugged. "I don't mind a broken arm. It's a soldier's lot to get shot at and clubbed by the foe, I guess. But whatever were you trying to do with that damned fifty-foot log or spar or whatever you call it? You almost killed me!"

Alec grinned, weakly. "With all those Indians and only one Rollo Gamble I figured the odds were pretty good I'd hit them and miss you. Anyway, it broke up the party, didn't it?"

Frenchy Villard grinned. *"Bien sur!* Make big noise, like cannon! I never see Bad Eye run that fast! They all follow him, jump over side, swim like alligator after them, by damn!"

"Now this is enough talk!" Nora exclaimed. "Rollo, you and the rest must go out and let Alec sleep to recover his strength."

Rollo! Already she called him Rollo! Alec turned his face to the wall, hearing the drying brown paper crackle. When they had all gone he rolled warily back. Nora Tobin was still sitting beside him. The glow of the candle lit her hair again in that unsettling way. Her eyes were dark pools in the shadows. She had pulled a flowered shift over her underwear, and he smelled perfume. Or was it just—Nora?

"Now you don't need to worry!" she soothed. "Sam Fat is at the wheel, and your uncle has everything well in hand."

"At least no one was killed," he said. Remembering the importance of time now, he asked, "What time is it?"

"Sundown, almost."

In a way, wearing only the simple shift and with the grime of battle smudging her cheeks, she resembled the old Nora, before Miss Waddell's school in Omaha. But he would not be deceived. Nora was only being kind to him.

"Alec?"

"I'm trying to sleep," he muttered.

"Oh, pooh! You're just being stubborn, like you always are when your nose is out of joint!" More gently she added, "I'd like to stay a little longer, if you're not in too much pain. I want to explain how I came to be on your boat, tell you how it came about. I owe you that much, I guess."

"You don't owe me anything, Miss Tobin."

"Miss Tobin! Now you're being childish! You know my name is Nora!"

He shrugged. "Nora, then!"

She looked down at the shift, smoothed wrinkles. "Goodness, I must look a sight!" She paused, seeming to search for words. "That night when you and Rollo—"

He winced again.

"Does your head hurt so?"

"It's all right. Go on."

"First," Nora said, seeming glad for the interruption, "I must pour some more vinegar on that paper! It's drying out!"

Some of it trickled into a corner of his mouth and he made a face. "Aagh!"

"It's good for you," Nora said. "Well, to begin—"

"Wait a minute!" Alec rose on one elbow. "What's that?"

"What's what?"

"The engine has stopped!"

In spite of her attempt to restrain him Alec tottered from his cot and stumbled to the engine room aft. Hugh Munro was shutting down the main steam valve and banking his fires. It was dusk. *Rose of Dundee* was snubbed against the bank.

"What the hell's going on?" Alec demanded.

"Nephew! What are you doing here? You're supposed to be in bed with a broken pate!"

Alec propped his hand against the doorjamb for support. "Never mind that! Open the valve and fire up again! Whose idiotic idea was it to lay to like this?"

"We're practically out of wood," Hugh insisted, "and Sam Fat is afraid to go any farther in the dark! Lieutenant Gamble said we'd better stop, too, and try to find wood in the morning and make up the time we lost today."

"Who's captain of *Rose of Dundee?*" Alec shouted. "Unless we pull out of here and steam upriver, the deck will be full of Sioux again at three o'clock tomorrow morning!"

"There's naught but a few sticks of wood, Alec!"

Alec remembered the splintered spar lying on the foredeck.

"Saw up that broken spar! Burn whatever you can find—but let's keep going!" He turned, went uncertainly forward, holding on to things, and made his way up the ladder. Lord, how his skull hurt! Could a bit of brain be seeping out of a crack?

Sam Fat had gone below. Rollo Gamble and Frenchy were in the pilothouse. Rollo, one-armed, had his carbine resting on the sill of the broken window and was scanning the dark forest. Frenchy was dabbing at blood that seeped from his wounded arm.

"Oho! What you do here, Alec? You *malade*—sick!"

"I'm all right." Alec spoke into the brass tube. "Give me half astern as soon as you've got a capful of steam, uncle!"

Rollo grounded the carbine with a bang. "You mean you're going to steam upriver at night?"

"Yes."

"You told me it was too dangerous!"

"I'm not reliable," Alec said crisply.

"There's no wood, either!"

"Enough to go a few miles before Bad Eye and his Sioux

fall on us again." Alec pointed to a faint latticing of silver on the foredeck, the silhouettes of stacks, shadows of stays. "There's a moon—that'll help."

They backed down, headed again into the main current. Alec peered into the darkness, pressing his memory. Was that Goat Head, the dim bulk to port? But there was a similar outcropping at Blazer Bar, and the river was dangerously shoal there. Steamers had to reach far to starboard, creeping around the wooded point to avoid the treacherous bottom. For a while there had been a gold camp, with shacks built of lumber salvaged from paddle-wheelers come to grief.

He rang for five revolutions, trying to make up his mind. Goat Head, or Blazer Bar? Although the river had returned to something near normal, the June rise had changed its face. Licking his lips with his tongue, he estimated the direction of the wind on his face through the broken glass, stared at the blackness. Blazer Bar, he decided.

Cautiously he maneuvered Rosie to starboard until he could almost feel the encroaching shore, smell the leaves on the darker bulk that were trees against a star-sprinkled heaven. Far away a coyote yipped, then another; the night filled with doglike cries.

From ahead came a small breeze. Even against the pounding of the engine he could sense deep water under Rosie's hull; the breeze meant that they had cleared the wooded point. That *had* been Blazer Bar; he had guessed right! He patted the oak wheel affectionately.

Uncle Hugh Munro's voice rasped through the speaking tube. "Nephew, there's enough wood for ten minutes more! All I've got left is a few sticks!"

"Burn them! I'll think of something!"

"Alec, *ami*—" Frenchy tugged at his sleeve.

"What is it?"

"She burn coal?"

"What are you talking about?"

"Rosie!" Frenchy insisted. "She burn coal?"

"She'd burn corncobs, I guess, if we had any!"

"You know *pa noo tsi ki na?*"

Alec stared at the woodhawk's bearded face, a pale smudge in the darkness of the pilothouse. He had a feeling that Frenchy was speaking some logical assemblage of English words, but more of Alec's battered brains must have leaked out.

"Know *what?*"

Frenchy struggled for words. "That Sioux name. Mean—" He pondered. "Plenty—coal. *Oui,* that it. Plenty Coal Bluffs, he name. You know—just up from Blazer Bar this funny hill black and white stripe like skunk? White some kind chalk, *je pense.* Black—he coal."

Alec sighed with relief; he was not yet feebleminded.

"Dig out," Frenchy explained, making shoveling motions with his hands. "Soft, dig out, burn in Rosie. Make lot smoke, but hot fire! Squaw mine used to dig, fry bacon with coal, make coffee."

They had just passed Blazer Bar. "You mean Zebra Hill?" Alec asked.

"They call Zebra too. That's *other* name!"

Plenty Coal Bluffs—Zebra Hill—must be dead ahead. Alec squinted into the blackness. The moon laid a silvery mist over everything, blurring detail as much as it revealed. Coal, easily-dug-out coal? He could put Sam Fat's coolies to work—digging, shoveling, bagging coal in gunnysacks, carrying the stuff down and dumping it on deck!

"I think—there," Frenchy said, pointing. Then, *"Merde, non!* Farther up, I think!"

In the silver-frosted dark Rosie groped her way. From the shore night birds called, disturbed in slumber by the paddle-wheeler's passing. The coyotes followed them along the bank. Frenchy and Gamble joined Alec in leaning out the broken windows.

"I think—" Frenchy mused. "I think—*oui,* by God, there she is—just like skunk, I say!"

Peering upward they could see the chalky cliff, make out the striated darker bands of coal. "Unhook her, uncle!" Alec called. "We're going ashore, all hands!"

With the discovery of fuel his head felt better. Jamming the vinegary brown paper hat tight, he scrambled down the ladder. In a nest of cordage Sam Fat slumbered, precious pigtail wound round his skull. Alec shook him awake.

"Get your men, Sam! Round up all the shovels and axes and knives and forks and spoons you can find—anything to mine coal!"

Sam's round face was puzzled. "Mine coal?"

"Sacks, too—gunnysacks, buckets, anything to carry coal! That's Plenty Coal Bluffs up there, and it's full of coal to stoke Rosie's boiler!"

Ben Bagley, sleepy-eyed, joined them. Nora Tobin, too, came from her cabin. "Coal? What's this all about?"

"You can go back to sleep, Nora," Gamble said. "We men have some coal mining to do before we can get any farther upriver."

Nora took the ribbon from her hair and tied it around the waist of the shift. "I'll help."

"You can't, Nora!" Gamble objected. "This is man's work."

She pulled a pair of Alec's old boots on her feet, straightened. "Pooh! I'm a strong healthy female! If there's work to be done, I'm entitled to my share!"

"But—"

"Save your breath," Alec advised. "If you caught leprosy she'd want a share."

Sam Fat roused his Oriental crew and shagged them out on deck. They stood bewildered, reeking of opium, while he passed down the line, handing out picks and shovels and gunnysacks. "You crowards, run away from Indians! Now you work, work hard, make up for crowards!"

"Cowards," Alec suggested.

"That right—crowards!" Sam Fat agreed. "Captain say too —you all crowards!"

Frenchy, arm too painful to dig coal, was left on *Rose of Dundee* as guard, along with Rollo Gamble. One paced a beat forward and the other aft. Cursing, pushing aside branches that threatened to poke their eyes out, slipping and falling on rain-wet slopes, falling into mudholes, the little band slogged up Zebra Hill. Nora, shoes sucking in the mud, trudged alongside Alec carrying a hoe. Alec held a lantern in one hand and a pick in the other.

"You shouldn't have come, you know," she said.

He was silent.

"You should be back on board Rosie, resting!"

He said nothing. It was all after the fact, anyway. When he tried to help her over a rocky ledge she pushed his hand away. "You needn't help me. I'm perfectly capable!"

The moon emerged from a rack of clouds. Before them lay the great cliff, banded with coal. In the moonlight the chalk layers shone with ghostly brilliance. What did Frenchy call it—*pa noo tsi* something? Among the river pilots there was a belief that the cliff was sacred to the Sioux, that they climbed atop it and threw down nubile Indian maidens. Somehow, in the moonlight, it did look haunted by spirits.

"All right," Alec said. "This is it! Let's start digging! Sam Fat, form your men into a bucket brigade to carry the stuff down to the boat! Stow it anywhere there's room—on deck, in the bilges, even in the cabins if you have to. We've got to have fuel—lots of it!"

All night they labored by the light of lanterns, backs aching, hands torn and bleeding. Soon they were covered with dust that the dampness turned into something like black paint. Nora labored as hard as anyone, and became grimy and disheveled. Alec worried about her. Lugging a sack of coal, he paused by the seam she was hacking.

"Nora, for God's sake go down to the boat and wash up! You look like a blackamoor! Besides, that kind of stooping and bending and lifting heavy loads isn't good for a woman's—a woman's—well, it isn't good for the female organs!"

She straightened, wiping a dirty hand across a previously marble brow. With a rag she had bound up her hair in a kind of turban. It slipped over one eye, giving her a distinctly raffish look. She had not spoken, but when he turned away, sighing, she called after him. "Are you all right, Alec?"

"I'm all right," he said. But he wasn't. An iron band was tightening about his temples. He forced himself to move cautiously with the heavy sack, bracing himself for each step, not wanting to betray himself by a fall.

Dawn flushed the sky with pinks and mauves as they lugged the last sack down the slope and dumped it on Rosie's deck. Uncle Hugh, looking like a black imp from Hades, stared sadly about.

"Poor old girl!" he quavered. "My Lord—Rosie looks like an Edinburgh whore!"

In the growing light of dawn *Rose of Dundee* was a sad sight. Her decks, once scrubbed until the oak planks showed white, were piled high with coal—coal in sacks, coal in buckets, coal piled in makeshift bins, coal piled in cabins and falling out of open doors. Rosie's stern wheel lacked several blades and the starboard spar was gone. A stay had been cut by a Sioux hatchet and one of the stacks teetered drunkenly. During the melee a post supporting the hurricane deck had been dislodged; now a large portion sagged low, almost touching the gunwales. The windows in the pilothouse had been shot out, along with many windows on the main deck, and arrows studded Rosie's woodwork. The boiler-plate armor was pocked with bullet scars, and the stern-wheeler listed to port from the weight of water she had taken on when no one had had time to man the pumps. But they had coal!

"Never mind," Alec said. "We'll make it up to the old girl some day!" He turned to Rollo Gamble. "Any sign of Bad Eye and his rascals?"

"Eh?" Gamble asked.

Alec's head hurt again; everything was becoming hazy. Blurred vision or not, he observed that Rollo Gamble had been interrupted from a pleasurable viewing of Nora Tobin. Nora had hiked the shift around her waist for better coal mining, and her décolletage was somewhat skewed.

"I asked," Alec said belligerently, "if you saw any sign of Bad Eye and his people while we were up on the cliffs!"

Gamble drew close to peer at him. "Are you all right? You're pale as a ghost, Alec! Even under that smut you—"

Alec teetered, then, and would have fallen except for Sam Fat's stout arm under his.

"You sick," Sam advised. "Better go cabin, sreep."

"Sleep," Alec muttered. "Yes, for some reason I—I'm a little unsteady."

Ben Bagley cleared coal from a cabin. Someone else let him gently down into bed. He did not sleep, but felt queer and disoriented. Now it must be near daylight; Sam Fat could handle the wheel. Tuesday, was this—or Wednesday? The seventh, the eighth of June? Or later? When he tried to figure, his brain seemed a bowl of porridge. But they had to reach Fort Mahone by the twelfth! When he tried to rise to explain it, his limbs refused to respond. With a groan he fell back on the coal-dirty pillow.

Once he opened his eyes to stare at the flickering candle. Someone sat by his bed. He could not focus well enough to make out who it was. But the person molded the paper cap about his throbbing skull again and he smelled the acrid tang of vinegar.

"I'm fine!" he protested. "Nothing wrong with me, nothing at all! In a minute I'm going to roll out and start Rosie upriver again! I'm—I'm—"

There was no reason why he was not perfectly able to finish the sentence, but his voice failed him; all the starch seemed to drain from his bones. He wanted to shout, to scream, to make everyone know that *Rose of Dundee* had to make Fort Mahone by the twelfth. But the person pushed him gently down on the soiled pillow, and he slept.

Chapter Six

When Alec woke he sat suddenly erect, feeling guilty. What was he doing sleeping? There were duties, neglected duties, as master of *Rose of Dundee*. But the engine was popping reassuringly; Sam Fat was probably at the wheel.

The time was late afternoon. In the gloomy cabin he would not have known except that someone drew the curtains and he blinked in the sunlight. "Hugh?" he asked, listening to the steady clamor of the exhaust.

It was not his uncle. It was Nora Tobin. She carried a tin tray. On it were roasted meat, eggs, and a steaming pot of coffee. He had thought they were out of coffee, but she seemed to have located some.

"No, it's not Hugh Munro," she said cheerfully. "It's me! How do you feel, Alec?"

Suddenly he remembered; the Sioux raid, Plenty Coal Bluffs, the all-night toil, the way his head hurt. Someone had put him to bed, taken off his pants and shoes, and then—

"I said—how do you feel?"

"All right, I guess," he muttered. "What are *you* doing here? And where are my pants?"

"I'm a passenger on your boat, remember? A paying passenger."

"You're not required to cook," he objected, sniffing the aroma.

"Oh, pooh! I'm a good cook. I can cook, sew, mine coal, do whatever I'm called on to do—if I want to, that is. Whatever else men may think, women are free creatures and have rights. You sometimes forget I have a mind of my own."

"I wonder," he said waspishly, "after you've given me so many pieces of it!"

She disregarded his humors. "Mr. Villard went ashore in the dinghy—is that what you call it?—and gathered duck eggs from the sandbars where they nest. He shot some ducks, too. I'm fixing roast duck for dinner. Mr. Sam Fat is trolling a line from the back part of your boat—"

"The stern!"

"Anyway, he caught quite a lot of fish, so I guess none of us will starve, though I must say your galley looks very bare."

While he ravenously ate the meat and the tough duck eggs, Nora watched. She had bathed, done up the taffy hair in a bright ribbon, and put on a silk dress with vaguely Japanese-looking scenes.

"The other night we were talking. I wanted to explain to you why I sneaked aboard Rosie, but when the engines stopped you ran out and there hasn't been a chance since."

He didn't want to hear about it, but his mouth was too filled with leathery duck eggs to protest. Too, he was concerned about the whereabouts of his pants.

"Alec, life is hard for a female! People expect her to get married at eighteen, and when she doesn't they say she's an old maid! Well, I don't intend to be an old maid, but I needed time to think! And there was Father pressing me so hard to marry Julius Winkle! It would be an excellent marriage, he kept saying. 'Julius is a fine man, with stock in the company and a promising career on the river.' Some day, Father said, Julius would inherit Missouri Packet Lines, and we two could carry on the company in Father's memory and leave it some day to our own children. You know the line means everything to Father!"

"I know," Alec said.

She poured a few drops of vinegar on the brown paper cap, paying no attention to his wrinkled nose.

"Suddenly that night—seeing you and all—I realized I didn't know *what* I wanted! I wasn't ready to get married to anyone!

Father was so angry when I told him I didn't want to go through with the engagement that I decided to run away. Bessie told me how she overheard you and Rollo were planning to steal *Rose of Dundee,* and—"

"You can't steal your own boat!"

"Well, anyway, I was frantic! I had to get away, and *think!* So I made up my mind to sneak aboard while you were loading cargo so I could visit my Aunt Belle Goggins—Father's sister—at Turkey Flats. Aunt Belle always took my part when Mama died. She and Father never got along, even when they were children. The last letter I got from her she said Father was a money-mad old fool, and hoped I'd not let him bully me."

Alec could not imagine anyone bullying Nora Tobin. However, with his headache waning, and his stomach filled with meat and eggs, he tended to feel magnanimous.

"I can understand your feelings."

"But now," Nora went on, twisting a handkerchief in the way she had when she was worried, "I'm more in a dither than before. I'm here with you, Alec, almost like old times, and it feels nice. What's a girl to do?"

Alec was indignant. "Why, Nora Tobin, you're collecting a regular harem, if you could say that about a female! Sparking Rollo Gamble, buttering me up, engaged to Julius Winkle—"

"I broke that up—for now, anyway!"

"Remembering old times, is it? Well, I want you to know I remember old times too, my girl! I kissed you once, in a boat on Wicket's Branch of a Sunday morning! You packed a picnic lunch—cold chicken and a bottle of your pa's wine you snitched. I remember we drifted along in the boat while you sang, and played the mandolin; "My Love Is Like a Blue-eyed Daisy," it was. You wore a dress with a red sash, and a straw hat. Your face was kind of hidden under the hat, and when I leaned over to—to—"

"To—what, Alec?"

Betrayed by emotion, he could only stammer. "I—I don't know. I don't remember what."

"You do too," she said. "You bent over to kiss me."

"I guess so," he said lamely.

She was silent, twisting the handkerchief. He glanced covertly at her, suspecting mistiness in her eyes to match his own. Nora—the old Nora, before she went to Miss Waddell's school in Omaha—never cried, even when she was helping him nail down warped deck planks on *Rose of Dundee* and hit her thumb with the hammer.

"And now," he said, "there's a new scalp at your belt, in a manner of speaking! Lieutenant Gamble! Rollo, as you call him very familiarly!"

"*You* call him Rollo!"

"That's different. I'm a man."

"Oho! That gives you lief, and not me, I suppose!"

"Well—"

"Rollo Gamble," she said, "is a very well turned-out gentleman! He's educated, too, with a distinguished career as a lawyer and an army officer, though he's only about ten years older than me. He can even speak French. A girl might do a great deal worse than marry Rollo P. Gamble." She hesitated. "I guess I should tell you he's already declared his intentions toward me to be strictly honorable and very serious."

"But you hardly know him!"

"That's not important when two hearts beat as one."

"Speaks French, does he? Well, I'll bet he doesn't know a blithering word of Gaelic, that was here long before talking-through-your-nose French! Besides, though I haven't been to college, I've read a lot. Maybe that fop Gamble has had a distinguished career, as you claim, but I haven't exactly been idle! Not to be boastful, I'm the lightningest pilot on the river, as everyone knows. Some day, when I get over this run of bad luck, I'll have my own fleet and run Missouri Packet Lines right off the river!"

"That's the most words you ever spoke to me in one run," Nora said. "Go on."

"So Gamble is romantic! Well, I'm romantic too, Nora Tobin! I know they say the Scots are phlegmatic, but fires can burn deep down inside, you know! That kind of a fire can be hotter and longer-lasting than some flashy little poof on the surface!"

She stopped fussing with the handkerchief and stared at him. "Alec—does your fire burn for me, really?"

"That was just a figure of speech," he said sheepishly. "What I was trying to say—"

"Good old Alec!" Her jaw set, and she shook her head. "That's what I expected! A figure of speech! No real meaning to it at all!"

"I *did* mean it!" he protested. "Listen—"

"I will not listen to any more of your Highland ravings! I came here to talk to you, to tell you my problems! I am a confused and lonely female—there, I admit it! All I was doing was trying to set my course in life with the aid of an old friend. But you don't understand. You just don't understand!"

Indignant, he stared at her.

"Maybe I do understand! And what I'm beginning to understand is that you're a flibbertigibbet, Nora Tobin—a heartless creature toying with men's lives! Let me tell *you* something! I hadn't got around to speaking of it, but Julius Winkle's damned *Sultan* is steaming upriver after us right now, so you're going to have to make a decision pretty soon! Your pa is on board too, so Ben Bagley told me. They're both madder 'n hell—" He was sorry about the profanity, but pressed on. "They're real mad and they hope to catch up with us and put me in jail and thrust you into the arms of Julius Winkle whether you want to or not! *I* think it would serve you right!"

In sudden concern she pressed the scrap of lace to her lips. "Oh, no!"

"It's a fact! Now you see the truth of the old saying—'Oh,

what a tangled web we weave when first we practice to deceive!'" He had been spinning a pretty tangled web himself, but did not mention it.

"Don't let them!" she begged. "Alec, I—I must have time to think this out! It's—it's my whole life I have to decide on! Help me!"

"It's my life too!" he reminded her. "It's even that oily Julius Winkle and Rollo Gamble that you're dangling on your string, Miss Nora Tobin!"

She rose, and in a sudden gale of passion ripped the handkerchief to shreds. Her eyes, normally cornflower-blue, darkened to the shade of a gun barrel.

"All right!" she cried. "I don't need your help anyway! From this time on our acquaintance is at an end! You are to forget me totally and completely, Alec Munro, and I will extend the same courtesy to you! Whatever happens, I am responsible for my own fate and no one else's! You sail your ship and I will sail mine!" Fixing him with a look that would have chilled a side of beef, she flounced from the cabin.

"Nora!" Alec called. There was no answer, only the slamming of the door. The remains of a broken pane tinkled musically as it fell out onto the deck.

"All right then!" Alec shouted after her. "But don't forget me so much you don't pay me eighteen dollars for passage to Turkey Flats!" He mopped his forehead. "Stubborn female!" he muttered under his breath, and found his pants.

They were all gathered in the pilothouse—Frenchy, Rollo Gamble, Ben Bagley with a nosebag of feed for his roan mare. Sam Fat was at the wheel, perplexed. "Which way?" he muttered, staring at the many river channels before him. "Do' know!"

"Starboard!" Alec commanded. "Good Lord, haven't I managed to pound anything into your pigtailed skull?"

They turned in surprise, relieved when he took the wheel

from the Chinaman. "Alec? You all right, boy?" "How's your head?" "Sure you can handle her now?"

"That's Jenkins' Chute ahead," he told Sam Fat. "It's impossible to steam right through there; the current's too fast. What you do, you ring down the engine and coast around that snag. Then when you're clear, you go full ahead and scoot right over the bar with the rusty boiler sitting on it. Don't you remember? That's where the old *Ace of Hearts* ran aground two years ago." To the rest of the company he said, "Sure, I'm all right. I just had quite a brannigan. There's nothing like a good fight to clear the head."

"A fight?" Rollo Gamble asked. "With who?"

Alec disregarded the question. "By God!" he muttered. "The damned river has dropped another foot!" He closed his eyes, turning the wheel a degree this way and that, smelling, hearing, feeling the river. "There can't be more than a fathom underneath Rosie's bottom!"

"Drop damn low!" Sam Fat agreed. "Be that way all morning. Where water go anyway? Must be leak in river!"

Uncle Hugh Munro's voice shrilled from the bell of the speaking tube. "Alec, is that you up there? What the hell are you doing on your feet?"

"I'm all right," Alec answered. "Be ready to give me full ahead when I call for it, uncle!"

A hundred yards ahead the Yellowstone narrowed, seemed to dip into a hidden chasm swirling with foam. To one side lay a stretch of shallow water; they could see "sawyers"—hidden snags—below. Still sliding forward, though the engine was idling with only an occasional gruff snort, *Rose of Dundee* slowed, yawing as she began to lose way. Vagaries of the current began to press her into the shallow water and away from the foaming chute. Sam Fat's moon face paled.

"Cap, better you—"

"Shut up!" Alec advised. "Can't you see I'm busy? Now watch!"

Eyes narrowed against the afternoon sun, they watched the

deadly snags come closer. Ben Bagley shifted his feet. Frenchy muttered something in French that sounded vaguely religious. Rollo Gamble took a deep breath, coughed.

"Now!" Alec shouted. "Full ahead, uncle!"

The idling engine burst into sudden clamor. Paddles washed, throwing up such gouts of water that spume drifted through the broken windows of the pilothouse. Rosie trembled like a hunter approaching a jump.

"Go it, girl!" Alec yelled. "Go it, now!"

Decking vibrated with the full power of the engine. The exhaust roared, a last shard of glass fell from a broken window. Frenchy stepped hastily away from the sill. *"Mon dieu*—we blow up?"

Running full speed at the bar, Alec barely missed the rusting boiler of the *Ace of Hearts*. Sand gritted along the keel and Rosie slowed, but only for a moment. With a last effort she dragged herself across Dead Man's Bar and glided into deep water.

"Throttle her down, uncle!" Alec called.

Once more they chuffed up the river, only broad sun-dappled reaches ahead. Ben Bagley clapped Alec on the back. "Neat as ever I seen done! I'm glad you're back, son! Now I got to give Pepperpot her grub. The mare gets put out when I'm late."

Alec turned the wheel back to Sam Fat. He felt better now, but his legs seemed made of India rubber. For a moment he looked at them, his river companions. They resembled pirates. Ben had a scabbed cut on his cheek from a Sioux hatchet and the seat of his pants was torn out. Frenchy's gray-fuzzed chest was striped with Sioux paint where he had grappled with one of Bad Eye's braves; the bloody bandage spiraled around his upper arm. Rollo Gamble still clutched the carbine, but the other limb, in rude splints, depended from a sling. The dress blues the lieutenant had worn to entertain Nora Tobin on the foredeck would never be the same. One sleeve was torn away, an epaulet probably now graced the shoulder of a Sioux brave, and a leg of the trousers was rent to show a hairy muscular calf. Neither had Sam Fat escaped. In the melee he had lost a good half of his precious queue, and he had a spectacular black eye.

"You're one hell of a looking bunch!" Alec grinned. "But I'm bound to give you good marks for spunk!"

Rollo Gamble picked up his dividers and went to the chart table. "My God!" he said. "Do you know how far we've got to go yet?"

"I've lost track."

"According to my calculations we're still two hundred miles from Fort Mahone, and it's only three more days till the twelfth of June!"

Alec picked up the dividers, scaled off the rambling course of the river. "By the chart, yes. But with all the backing and filling we've probably got to do, it's probably farther."

"Then you've got to run at night! All night! Every night! Even then I don't know if we can make it!"

The sun seemed to pave the river with cobblestones of gold. Along the banks Alec could see the old waterline; the river was now a good foot or so below that mark.

"It's risky," he said.

"But the other night—"

"We had to press on then," Alec explained. "If we hadn't, Bad Eye and his people would have caught up with us. We'd all be going around barefoot on top of our heads."

Gamble blinked. "Say that again?"

"Old frontier expression. It means 'scalped.'"

Gamble picked up the dividers and drove them into the soft wood of the chart table. "You mean you're giving up, then?"

Every Sunday it was his rule to hold Presbyterian services on the boiler deck for all hands, even the uncomprehending Chinese, reading from his father's old Bible. In view of his devoutness, why had God put him in such a position? All he had ever wanted was to run the river in his own vessel. That limited world was all he ever asked for. Now he had become a fugitive from justice shouldering an impossible task—take a hundred tons of military cargo in an impounded boat up to Fort Mahone near the head of navigation; two hundred miles, it now figured, in three days, on a river that seemed intent on drying up under him. Not only that, he must contend with murderous Red Indians and a fractious female. His pockets were empty; even if some of the woodhawks returned to the river after the Sioux scare, he had no money to buy fuel. Besides all else, Julius Winkle's *Sultan* was behind him, chasing him with a furious Horace Tobin and a vengeful skipper.

"Well?" Gamble prodded.

When he undertook the task he had been rash, no two ways about that. He had talked glibly about driving his beloved Rosie to the bottom of the Yellowstone rather than let Horace Tobin have her. Still and all, when the time came—

"I'm thinking," he muttered.

He stepped gingerly out on the hurricane deck, keeping well to the rail so he would not slide off and be pitched into the water. With deep emotion he stared down at Rosie. Gallant lady! Sore wounded, *Rose of Dundee* nevertheless plodded doggedly on. *She* was trying; could he do less?

Going back into the pilothouse, he felt renewed. "Give up?" he asked Gamble. "Is that what you were hinting at?"

"Stop bandying words!" the lieutenant snapped.

"No, we're not giving up," Alec said. "It's not in my nature, and certainly not in Rosie's." He called into the bell of the speaking tube. "Uncle, give me twenty revolutions!"

Hugh Munro's voice sounded uncertain. "It's getting late, nephew. Hadn't we better be looking for an anchorage?"

"Twenty revolutions, and hang the anchorage!" Alec cried. "We're not going to stop as long as there's a lump of coal left!"

Through the watches of the night he remained at the wheel, scanning the outline of the river. The moon was almost full and the Yellowstone glowed with soft radiance. Hugh Munro, without Alec's youth, fell asleep and could not be roused by the speaking tube. Rollo Gamble ran below and finally roused the old man.

On through the night they bored, occasionally scraping bottom, once going full aground. In accordance with Alec's orders Gamble roused the coolies. They put a chain over the side and stretched it under the vessel to break the suction. Standing shoulder-deep in water on both sides of *Rose of Dundee*, they dragged the chain from bow to stern. With Rosie's engine at a dangerous pressure and embers shooting from her stacks like Roman candles, enough sand was washed away so that the paddle-wheeler slipped free. Accelerating, Rosie glided ahead, leaving the Chinamen astern, shouting Cantonese distress. Alec backed down and they clambered aboard, jabbering.

"An interesting technique," Gamble commented. "I only hope your good friend Captain Winkle is not so clever!"

Alec snorted. "That bag of wind is a fair-weather skipper! All he knows is the old ladies' run up the Missouri to Fort Benton! Right now I'd bet he's stuck on a bar back at Rainy Butte!" But he did not feel as confident as he sounded. Julius Winkle was cunning; you had to give him that. Besides, *Sultan* would be running unloaded, drawing little water, and her two big low-pressure engines more than matched Rosie's one-lunger.

Morning came, and with it a bright sun and a following breeze that gave Rosie an extra knot or so. Alec, beard stubbled and eyes red, gave the wheel over to Rollo Gamble and dozed on the stool, shoulders wedged in a corner of the pilot-house. He did not even hear the popping of the exhaust. If it had stopped he would have awakened instantly. Now he slept, the ear-splitting noise almost a lullaby.

When he woke the sun was well past the zenith. Cottonwoods along the bank cast lacy shadows on the water. Yawning, he resumed the wheel. The scene was peaceful, almost idyllic. Birds sang; Alec crooned soft instructions to Rosie as he swung the wheel this way and that.

"A little to starboard now, sweetheart. That's right—easy!

Now we'll just pay off a little to miss that snag, and swing back again. Nicely done!"

Now that the crest had passed, some downriver traffic resumed. Mackinaws went by, wooden scows steered with long sweeps by their proprietors, carrying furs, high-grade ore, and miscellaneous cargo. A work-boat anchored in the shallows with a military engineer squinting through a surveyor's transit while blue-shirted enlisted men rested on their oars. The proprietor of a woodyard held up his crudely lettered sign GOOD RIVVER OKE AND BULL PINE ONLY FIVE DOLLAR $ CORD. His Indian woman washed clothing in the river, shading her eyes with a hand to watch the first paddle-wheeler in weeks.

Aware of another presence in the pilothouse, Alec turned. Nora Tobin stood in the doorway. In her arms was a large tortoiseshell cat, purring as she stroked its fur. She wore a new frock of palest pink, girded with a golden chain.

"Well!" he said unpleasantly. "I thought our acquaintance was at an end!"

She ignored him, speaking instead to the furry bundle in her arms. "Does precious see the wheel? That's where the man steers the boat, do you see? And there's the tube he talks down to the engine room with. The thing on the stand there—that's the compass. It tells the captain where to go."

Remembering his pilothouse recently overflowing with cats, Alec was annoyed. "Where did that damned animal come from?"

Nora looked at him in blue-eyed innocence. "Sir, are you speaking to me?"

"Don't act precious, Nora! You know I am!"

"Well," she said, "since I see you are attempting to renew our relationship, I suppose I must be charitable. Rollo—Lieutenant Gamble, that is—took Baby here from one of his crates when he saw me admiring her."

"Baby? Good Lord!"

"Isn't she a beauty, though? Such a sleek coat, and her eyes are soft brown, like—like—"

"Like Rollo Gamble's, I suppose!"

She went on stroking the cat's back.

"Well, no cats in the pilothouse!"

She sniffed. "If a little cat upsets you so—"

"No visitors, either! In the pilothouse, I mean!"

She was annoyed. "Everyone else comes up here! I don't see why I can't!"

"You're only a passenger," he said. "The others all had legitimate business."

"Pooh! You're just being stuffy."

Narrowing his eyes, he squinted into the afternoon glare. What was that ahead—the faraway dark line across the Yellowstone? Bracing a knee against the wheel to hold Rosie steady, he picked up his spyglass, rotating the brass barrel. The image was hazy and indistinct even with the glass. Still, there was something there, something that didn't belong.

"Whatever are you muttering about?" Nora demanded. "Speak up, Alec!"

The image sharpened, became distinct.

"All right then, you old grouch! If that's the way you want to act—"

"Quiet!" he snapped.

She was angry. "Don't you tell me to be quiet, Alec Munro! I—" Seeing his fixed attention ahead, she broke off. "Alec, what is it?"

Rosie was closing fast on the obstacle. Now Alec knew what it was. A giant fir had fallen across their way. While the riverbed had been plowed by the great rise into myriad side-channels, only the central one appeared to contain enough water to accommodate Rosie's hull—and that central channel was blocked.

Rollo Gamble ran out from under the sagging hurricane deck, cupping his hands to yell at Alec. "There's a tree across the river! Do you see it?"

Excited, clamoring, the Chinese crowded the bow, pointing.

From the steamy engine room Hugh Munro came, mopping a sweating face. "What's all the babble about?"

Ben Bagley joined the group, and Frenchy Villard. "Up there!" the woodhawk yelled. "Big, big tree, Alec! *Sacre bleu—* what we do, eh?"

Now they were near the fallen giant. The farther outreaches of the branches brushed against *Rose of Dundee*'s superstructure. Odd—the tree looked healthy enough. Perhaps the rains had loosened its roots. Now they would have to chop their way through the trunk with axes; two or three hours delay at the best!

Alec leaned out the window. "Uncle, secure the engine! Sam Fat, see that Rosie's properly moored to the tree with the bow line. Then get all the saws and axes you can find and send your crew up on that damned tree to hack it through!"

Staring into a needled recess of the great tree, he bit his words short. Leering back at him was a bearded face crowned with a tattered felt hat.

"And where," Woolly Willie Yates demanded, "is that sneaky conniving coyote Hugh Munro that cheated me at draw poker?" Holding up the ax with which he must have felled the tree, Willie looked about. "There you are, you old scoundrel!"

With an agility surprising in so big a man he jumped to the foredeck, locking a burly arm around the startled Hugh Munro's neck. Pressing the shining blade of the ax against Hugh's quivering Adam's apple, he grinned. "Hugh Munro, I'm going to chop your scheming head off and use it for a float on my catfish line! *That*'ll teach you a lesson!"

Chapter Seven

For a moment there was silence, in part because of Woolly Willie's arboreal appearance, but in greater part from the immediate threat to Uncle Hugh Munro's grizzled head. Alec was the first to find his voice.

"Willie," he said, "turn him loose! Can't we talk this over?"

Ben Bagley stepped forward also, raising a placating hand. "Now, Willie, cool down! Remember the last time I let you out of jail? You promised to obey the law. Cutting a man's head off is against the law!"

Uncle Hugh Munro tried to speak, but his wind was cut off. All he could do was to make squeaking noises and nod in agreement. But when Sheriff Bagley approached, Willie's yellow horse-teeth bared in a snarl. Experimentally he sawed the edge of the ax against Hugh's throat. "Back!" he warned. "Stay back, all of you!" His keglike neck swelled in passion. "I didn't ride all the way up here through mud and high water and Sioux Indians just to palaver!" He raised his nose high and howled like a wolf. "I—want—justice!"

Willie had had a varied career in the East before arriving in the Territory for his health. That health, it was rumored, had been improved by escaping a hempen noose in Tennessee for killing a man by throwing an iron cookstove at him. Willie was dangerous, there was little doubt of that. At the moment he was in the grip of a passion that could make him capable of any barbarity.

For once Rollo Gamble was without the company of his carbine. Broken arm in a sling, he looked about for a weapon and picked up a stick of lumber from the wreckage of the sagging hurricane deck.

"Don't, Rollo!" Alec warned. "Here—give me that!" He snatched the scantling from Gamble and advanced on Woolly Willie. "You're choking him to death!" he protested. "Damn it, Willie—turn him loose! He's blue in the face!"

Willie pressed hard with the razorlike blade. Hugh, only half conscious, cried out in pain. Alec, fearing that his uncle would perish before his eyes, rushed forward, swinging the stick. Willie dropped his grasp on Uncle Hugh. Wresting the club out of Alec's hand, he kicked him in the stomach. Alec slid halfway across the littered deck, ending up in a pile of coal which fell down, half covering him.

Dazed, he watched as Frenchy and Ben Bagley and Sam Fat attacked Willie, who stood over Hugh Munro like a colossus, throwing the rescuers back with regularity. Frenchy skittered beside Alec into the coal pile, gasping for breath and clutching his wounded arm. "By damn!" he wheezed. "That Willie got arm like fence post!" Shakily he got to his feet. "You wait here," he advised. *"Je reviendrai!"*

Alec swayed to his feet. He remembered that Woolly Willie Yates had taught Nora to spit through her teeth when she was nine years old. Willie, hostler at the Springer's Landing livery stable, had also, until old Horace found out, shown Nora how to shoot a pistol and to chew tobacco. Willie's tutoring was successful with the exception of the tobacco chewing. Nora got sick, throwing up in her father's parlor; the secret of her frequent absences leaked out.

"Nora!" Alec looked frantically about. Maybe Nora could prevail on the maddened giant. But how like a female—never around when you wanted her! "Nora!" he bawled. "Goddamnit, come here, will you?"

Frenchy returned quickly to the coal pile, rolling into it with a groan. Ben Bagley sat on deck holding his head. Sam Fat, the remnant of his pigtail in Willie's grasp, yelled for his countrymen to help him. Fearing violence, however, the

Chinamen had bolted to the bilges. Rollo Gamble, cursing his broken arm, tried to remember where he had left his carbine. Willie leered.

"Now," he said, retrieving his ax, "I've got a little business to transact here." To Uncle Hugh Munro, who was crawling away, he said, "Come back, you little rat, and lay your scheming head on this here chunk of wood!" Reaching out, he caught Uncle Hugh by the trousers.

"Nora!" Alec screeched.

A crow flew low over the damaged foredeck, then soared away in fright at Alec's cry. But Nora Tobin, carrying Baby the cat, emerged from her cabin.

"My goodness!" she complained. "What is all this thumping and caterwauling about? I was just having a nap when—" Catching sight of the tableau, she paused. "My goodness! Mr. Willie, whatever are you doing here?"

Willie blinked in surprise.

"Please put down that ax!" Nora said in a firm voice. "Haven't you got any manners at *all?*"

"Ma'am?"

"I said put down that ax! Why, I don't know what's got into you! I never saw you act so before!"

Willie closed his eyes and opened them again as if Nora Tobin would disappear, only a wraith of his imagination. But Nora was still there. Willie's grip on Uncle Hugh Munro loosened, the fist holding the ax wavered.

"Miss Nora," he complained, "I don't think you understand. I—"

"I do too!" Carefully she put down Baby, who remained at her feet, rubbing her arched back against Nora's slender ankles. "You've been taken by a sudden fit of some kind, and now it's over!" With a shudder she snatched away the ax and handed it to Alec. "I *know* you wouldn't hurt a fly, Willie. You are a good and a kind man!"

Frustrated, Willie cried out. "Damn it—'scuse me, ma'am—this here rascal tried to cheat me in a game of draw poker at the Paradise Saloon! When he got lucky, I smelled a nigger in the woodpile. Sure enough—this here ring he was wearing had a little mirror built into the bottom of it! When he dealt the rascal saw every last card! I chased him out of the saloon and then—"

Nora made a clucking sound. "That was dishonest!"

"We looked high and low for him! All the barn lofts and rooftops, even amongst the coffins in Peebles' Funeral Parlor! Then I heard *Rose of Dundee* firing up, and I knew he'd got away. Ever since, I been riding my mule upriver on the old Hatcher wagon road. I got to Frenchy's place too late. I got to Zebra Hill too late. But now I got Hugh Munro dead to rights!" He turned to the company. "Ain't I entitled to maim him, at least?"

Alec cleared his throat, but Nora spoke first.

"So that's all it is! A gambling quarrel! Well, violence is no way to settle such matters! This may be the frontier, but we *are* civilized, aren't we?" She turned to the quaking Hugh Munro. "Uncle Hugh, you must tell Mr. Willie you're sorry!"

Hugh's eyes were glazed; his teeth chattered.

"Speak up!" Nora commanded. "I can hardly hear you!"

"I apologize," Hugh quavered.

Willie jammed hamlike fists into his pockets and kicked the deck. "Ma'am, it ain't hardly fair for that cockroach to get away with this! I seen men get their heads blowed off for less!"

Nora put a hand on his hairy arm. "Now that Uncle Hugh has apologized, you must shake hands with him!"

"Shake hands with that polecat?"

She pushed him forward, and took Uncle Hugh Munro's small paw. "This is the gentleman's way of handling such things." When their hands limply engaged, she stepped back, smiling. "I'm very proud of you both."

The late antagonists stood like statues, hypnotized by the course of events. When Alec spoke they jumped nervously and moved apart.

"Willie," Alec said, "we need your help! Lieutenant Gamble here has an important cargo aboard, a shipment of army goods that must be at Fort Mahone no later than day after tomorrow to supply a combined military operation. We're running late, and I know what you can do with that ax."

Willie eyed him cautiously.

"If you'll just climb up there and lay about, Willie, we can get that tree out of the way and steam upriver again."

"That's right," Nora agreed, picking up Baby. "Big and strong as you are, I'll bet you can outchop those Chinamen all by yourself, Mr. Willie."

"I don't know," Willie muttered. "I kind of intended to get some sleep and ride my old mule back to the Landing after I'd dealt with Hugh."

Nora was insistent. "There are evil forces trying to prevent Captain Munro from doing his patriotic duty! Mr. Willie, you must help us, as you once were so kind and helpful to me, only a child in my father's house."

Willie scratched a stubbly chin. "Evil forces?"

"Yes, indeed! Captain Winkle and his big boat *Sultan* are steaming after us, trying to stop us!"

"Julius Winkle? Nothing I'd like better than to put a spoke in *that* rascal's wheel!"

Nora had struck paydirt. She had always been more nimble-brained than Alec. With her quick tongue and an imaginative mind, she usually managed to outmaneuver him.

"It was up on the Missouri last summer," Willie said. "A pack of Crows come on me while I was running my trapline. Then Winkle's *Sultan* come by. I swum out far as I could, but I was that winded all I could do was hang on to a floating mine-timber and yell. Winkle saw me, I know he saw me! But he was in too much of a hurry to stop. Give me a toot on the whistle and steamed on, that's what the bastard—beg your pardon, ma'am—did!" Willie lifted the hem of his greasy deerhide shirt, exhibiting a scar. "I took a lance there before I finally got away." He bobbed his head apologetically. "Ain't polite to display my hide to no lady, but I just wanted you to know, ma'am, how I hate and despise Julius Winkle! I'll do anything if it will bollix *him!*" Seizing the ax, he clambered up on the tree. Dispossessing the Chinamen who had crept from the bilges, he swung the ax. Chips rained down. Faster and faster he chopped, Willie and the ax moving in synchronism like Rosie's slide valves and paddle-crank.

"Get ready to cast off!" Alec ordered Sam Fat. "Hugh, fire up!"

"Alec?" Woolly Willie peered over the greenery. "I disremembered. Solomon Two is over there in the bushes. We got to take him aboard."

"Of course, Willie. I'll have one of the Chinamen bring your mule aboard."

"No Chinamen," Willie warned. "He bites Chinamen!" He grinned, bushy eyebrows twitching. "Bit Julius Winkle once! Ruined a pair of St. Louis tailor-made pants for him!"

Alec waded ashore. Taking Solomon Two by the bridle, he managed to get the gray-muzzled mule to flounder aboard. A mule now, not to mention several crates of cats and Ben Bagley's roan mare chomping grass on the afterdeck! Rosie was beginning to look like a zoo!

"Company's come," Alec said to Pepperpot, tying Solomon Two to a stanchion beside her.

As he mounted the ladder to the pilothouse he was gratified to hear a crash, then a gurgling. The great tree, finally severed, dropped into the river.

He could hardly believe that the supply of coal they had laid in could dwindle so rapidly. Rollo Gamble, poring over the chart with his dividers, had an explanation.

"Eighty-two miles in twenty-four hours, I make it! We're running faster! By God, it's possible we can reach Fort Mahone in time, even with all the delays!" He made an entry in his notebook. "If," he added, "the damned river doesn't drop any more!"

Rollo's change of mood was well founded. The Yellowstone

had fallen so low that it looked like the infamous South Platte
—"a mile wide and a foot deep," as someone characterized that
river. Like the South Platte, the Yellowstone carried considerable water. But because of erosion caused by the great rise,
the water now flowed in broad shallow patches, almost lakes,
the main current's identity lost in chutes, side-channels, and
backwaters. Alec was taut with apprehension as he searched
for a course through the maze.

"Never fear," he said. "I've got a few tricks up my sleeve!"

Gamble leaned on the sill, rubbing the stiffened fingers of
his broken arm. "By God, she's a champion!"

Alec thought the lieutenant was talking about *Rose of Dundee*. "That she is," he agreed.

"Stood up to that ruffian Yates like a soldier!"

"Eh?"

"Miss Nora, I mean! A gallant lady. Beautiful, too! A
paragon of femininity—genteel laces and ribbons over Toledo
steel! Miss Tobin is made for a finer environment, like New
York City, where I understand my next duty station is likely to
be—Fort Suffolk. I see her at the opera, poetry readings, the
races at Saratoga! Paris frocks, riding about in a coach and
four—champagne, dancing the mazurka, arranging flowers in a
Japanese vase!"

"I don't know about all that," Alec said stiffly. "Remember,
she was born here! You don't know her as well as I do, either.
Nora's not your fancy type at all! Nora is a child of nature—or
was. She could ride when she was nine, and shoot the tops off
bottles at fifty feet. She never was afraid of snakes, and when
we went fishing she used to dig worms for me."

Gamble seemed not to listen. "When we get to Fort Mahone I daresay I'll have leave coming. Turkey Flats is only a
short ride from Fort Mahone. I don't mind telling you, Alec, I
intend to ask Aunt Belle Goggins if I may call on Nora."

"Do whatever you want when we get there," Alec blurted,
"but we've got to *get* there first!" He pointed to the western
sky, where a line of clouds drifted near the sun. "That's more

weather making up! Tonight there'll be no moon. Even by eating up the lights we'll be lucky to make good even five miles between sunset and sunup."

"Eating up the lights? What's that?"

"Something they don't teach in the Army!" Alec snapped.

He wiped his forehead with a tattered sleeve. While *Rose of Dundee* lay in Wicket's Branch he had sewed new gold braid on the cuffs and on his cap. Part of the braid had now been torn away; the rest was grimy with coal dust, and his captain's hat had no crown.

"You haven't eaten all day," Gamble said kindly. "I'll go below and rustle up some fried fish."

Alec's stomach was sour. "I can't eat," he muttered. "It would all come up anyway!"

Rollo looked searchingly at him. "You all right?"

"I'll make it. Just leave me alone, will you?"

Near dusk Sam Fat climbed the ladder with a tin plate of fried fish and a cup of watery coffee. "Lieutenant say you eat."

Alec swallowed hard, turned away. "Dump it over the side."

The Chinaman tossed the fish through the window and scrubbed the surface of the plate with a fold of his capacious sleeve. "You hard head like you uncle!"

"Don't sass me!" Alec reproved. "I'm in a bad mood!"

Sam Fat chuckled. "I know why, Cap!"

"What do you know, you damned heathen?"

The Chinaman retreated to the door, giggling.

"It won't be so funny," Alec warned, "when you go out in that boat tonight with an armload of candles!"

Sam Fat's moon face paled. "No!"

"Yes."

"I do' think so, I guess."

"I guess you will!" Alec pointed. "See those clouds? There won't be a glimmer of light tonight, and we've got to keep going!"

"Dark out there!" Sam Fat wailed. "L'il boat, water all round—there be devils, dragons, breathe fire and smoke!"

"You haven't seen fire and smoke till you see me snort up a conflagration," Alec told him. "Go below and get an armful of shingles and your candles, and the matches and all! Take one of your men to row the dinghy!"

"Prease?"

"No prease!" Alec said firmly. "You can't get round me, so stop trying! You *know* you're the only one! Hugh has to stay at the engines, and no one else has done it before."

Sam Fat retreated as Uncle Hugh's voice sounded from the engine room. "Alec, we're that low on coal!"

"How much?"

"At the knots we're making, another few hours. Say till midnight."

Alec made rapid calculations. Hugh continued. "Hadn't we better lay to, cut wood ashore?"

"There's not time! Remember, Winkle and his damned *Sultan* may be steaming up our wake any minute!"

"But—"

"I'm going to run at night!"

There was silence; then, Hugh's voice, incredulous. "I've just been out on deck for a breath of air! There's no moon, and the clouds look like rain! You'll lose Rosie, Alec!"

"I'm going to run the lights! Throttled down, we'll save a few hours of coal. By morning we should be up to Potter's Slough. I remember a stand of good bull pine there. We can lay to and chop wood—maybe enough to get us all the way to Fort Mahone without stopping."

Again there was silence. Then Hugh said, "Foosh! You're a damned fool, boyo! But I know better than to argue with you —about *anything!*"

In near blackness Alec rang down the engines so that *Rose of Dundee* was barely making headway. Beyond lay the Looking-Glass, always a shoal passage. He might lose Rosie, as Hugh predicted. But what else was there to do? If the *Sultan* caught up with them, they would impound *Rose of Dundee* and take him in irons to the jail at Springer's Landing; Rollo Gamble's military supplies would never reach Fort Mahone. And Nora—? He gritted his teeth. Gamble could court her at Springer's Landing as easily as at Turkey Flats. Alec Munro would languish in Ben Bagley's jail while the two lovers made plans for the opera. Alec swore a heartfelt Gaelic oath and leaned out the pilothouse window.

"Sam Fat?"

"Dragons!" a sepulchral voice wailed from the darkness below.

"Get into that dinghy and start!"

Rollo Gamble hurried up the ladder. "What's going on?" he asked.

"Watch!"

The night was as black as the inside of a cow. Rosie merely crept, the exhaust a murmur as the engine slowly turned.

"I don't see anything," Gamble protested.

"You will!"

Far ahead in the blackness a spark glowed. Alec turned the wheel. Rosie, responding sluggishly at such low speed, veered to starboard; the dim-lit compass card wavered a point, steadied.

"What's that light out there?" Gamble asked.

"Sam Fat, in the dinghy. He just lit the first candle." The spark glowed, strengthened, then went out. "Wind," Alec explained. "Blew out the candle."

"I don't understand," Gamble muttered.

The light came on again and Alec corrected the wheel. "We'd never get through here at night and probably not in daytime either without soundings. So Sam Fat goes ahead with shingles and an armful of candles. He takes soundings with a pole as the coolie rows. When they find passable water Sam Fat floats a candle on a shingle."

"Why don't they just drift downriver, or ashore?"

Alec spun the wheel a few degrees and peered into the darkness. More small lights bloomed. By now the slowly moving *Rose of Dundee* had run down the first light. It disappeared under the bows as candles glowed upriver.

"He ties a string to each shingle and fastens a rock to it to anchor it."

"That's ingenious!"

"I'm surprised you never heard of it. Didn't they learn you anything about boats at the Military Academy?"

"Boats are for Annapolis!" Gamble snapped. "I don't know anything about boats. I'm a cavalryman!"

Alec forgot everything else in his task. His hands clutched the wheel until they cramped and he had to loosen his grip to stretch his fingers. Rosie crept forward like a snail, engine throttled to a faint cough, paddles hardly splashing. Far ahead, Sam Fat continued to lay down a pathway of moored candles. Rosie continued to eat up the flickering lights. One floating candle escaped the paddles. When Rollo Gamble looked astern he saw the small spark behind them, bobbing in Rosie's wash.

"Missed one," he murmured.

"Plenty more ahead, unless a dragon eats Sam Fat and his boat."

Rosie slid gently over a bar, a grainy hissing coming from her brushed keel. From below came hollow groans. It sounded like the Greek chorus Alec once read about in a book Nora loaned him from her father's library. But Rosie's headway, small as it was, carried her over the bar and into deeper water.

"That was a close one," Gamble said.

The Looking-Glass was several miles in extent. It was nearing dawn when Sam Fat came back to the boat to report tolerable water ahead. Rollo Gamble looked ahead in the gray-streaked dawn, shook his head.

"Still doesn't look good to me! You mean Rosie's going to steam through that shallow puddle?"

In spite of his fatigue Alec grinned. "Friend, that's deep compared to what we just went over!"

Gamble's broken arm pained him. He released it from the sling and for a moment let it hang, but the rush of blood to the injured member made him bite his lip. "You're the captain," he said, "but with the river dropping lower and lower, maybe we're going to have to tie up soon and off-load my supplies— send someone on to Fort Mahone for horses and wagons. The roads are better now."

"That won't get the stuff there by the twelfth!"

The lieutenant's moustaches sagged. "I know."

"Trust me!" Alec said. "I didn't get those antlers on the pilothouse for nothing!"

Carefully Gamble thrust his arm back into the sling. The hand was swollen, fingers looking like brown sausages. "I've been meaning to ask you about the antlers."

"Means I'm the lightningest pilot on the Yellowstone," Alec said proudly. "Old Horace nominated Julius Winkle in the annual voting, and they stuffed the ballot box so Julius would win. So he got the official antlers, but everybody knew Julius Winkle was a fraud. A bunch of the independents, boats not beholden to Horace Tobin, got together and awarded me my own set." He squinted into the light rain starting to fall. "If I'm not mistaken, that's Potter's Slough ahead. We must be bare of coal by now." Calling for five revolutions, he turned the wheel. "We'll have to nose in here and cut wood. Above here there isn't much good stuff—nothing but willow and cottonwood and a lot of brush."

They entered a narrow channel, choked with bushes and scrub oak. At times the water seemed almost to disappear. There was a crackling and snapping as Rosie's bows pushed aside the green wall. But Alec had cut wood at Potter's Slough many times when the tin money box in the pilothouse had been empty.

"How the hell will you ever get out of this?" Gamble demanded.

"Back down! Rosie goes forward and backward!"

Finally the channel widened. Alec rang down the engine.

They moored in a great grove of pines, their ranks dotted with stumps where wood had been taken over the years. It rained, a misty drizzle. Alec shivered, drawing the tattered uniform coat tighter about him. "I'm that chilled!" he muttered. "I wonder if there's any coffee left?"

Sam Fat and Rollo Gamble organized the woodcutters. Frenchy Villard, in spite of his wound, picked up a bucksaw. Willie Yates tried to take it away, but Frenchy held on.

"You can't do no good with that hole in your hide," Willie pointed out.

"Saw with *bras gauche*—other arm!"

Ben Bagley approached Alec. One hand on his big stomach, he belched. "Alec, I'm through eating catfish! A man needs meat!"

It was true; there was no strength in fish, and they had been too hurried to land Frenchy for the deer watering along the banks.

"So," Ben said, "if you can spare me for a while, I'd like to take Pepperpot ashore and look for a nice fat buck." He licked his lips. "Fried deer steak—that's what makes a man's juices flow!"

Alec's own juices had run low. Exhausted, he slumped on the forward capstan. "All right," he agreed. "We've got plenty of people to chop, but they're not going to chop much unless we get something to stick to their ribs."

Eyelids drooping, he watched Nora Tobin come on deck. Somewhere she had found an old pair of jeans and a ragged shirt. Alec was scandalized at the way her hips filled the breeches. From the way her bosom moved about, she had on little in the way of nether garments. He was not familiar with ladies' underwear, but realized something was lacking.

"Where do you think you're going?" he grumbled. "Dressed like that, you're a sight for the jaybirds!"

She picked up the only tool left, a rusted hatchet. "Surely you don't expect me to chop wood in a long dress and petticoats?"

Nora had always been independent. Now she was impossible. He sighed, getting painfully to his feet.

"You're not going ashore?" she demanded.

He tried to take the hatchet from her, but swayed and sat down suddenly on the capstan.

"You're dead on your feet," Nora said quickly. "You stay here and get some sleep, Alec Munro!"

Feebly he reached for the hatchet, but she held it away. "You're the most obstinate man I ever knew! Are all Scots as pigheaded, or are you the champion in that field?" She got a hand under his arm and pulled him to his feet. "Now you just go in that cabin and get some sleep, do you hear me? Whatever would we do without you? What would we *all* do without you?"

He blinked. Was she crying again? Women were strange creatures. If there was anything else to marry, a man would be better off. But there you were—women, or nothing. In the long run, maybe nothing *was* better. Julius Winkle could have Nora. It would serve the scoundrel right. Or Rollo Gamble. Alec didn't care. He didn't care about anything. Rosie was his sweetheart; willing, faithful, not given to backtalk. Rosie was all he needed, and he had been foolish to divide his affections. He barely had strength to call a warning to Ben Bagley, who was mounting Pepperpot.

"Keep an eye peeled, Ben! Bad Eye and his people might still be lurking about!"

Now they were all gone; even Uncle Hugh had left his precious engine. *Rose of Dundee* lay silent except for an occasional meow and a sonorous breaking of wind from old Solomon Two, munching grass. The wood party had moved deep into the forest, the area near Rosie's mooring being nearly denuded of prime trees. Faintly Alec heard the sound of saws and axes, with an occasional faraway *whoosh* as a pine toppled. Shambling languidly toward a bed—any bed—he paused, hearing a strange sound. It seemed to come from the river.

Leaning against a stanchion, he screwed shut reddened eyes

and cupped a hand behind his ear. There it was again, borne on the wind through misty rain! *Sssoooo—hah! Sssoooo—hah!* Suddenly he knew that sound.

Hobbling to the port rail on stiff legs, he squinted through the screen of bushes. Potter's Slough paralleled the Yellowstone no more than a quarter mile inland. Through the screen of willow and scrub oak he saw movement. The scraps of vision quickly formed a dread image in his mind. Awkwardly he clambered over the rail toward the rain-soaked bank. Slipping and sliding in wet leaves, he made his way through the scrub, wincing as branches poked his eyes and tore his clothes. A snake slithered away, darting into the wet grass. Winded, he paused at the Yellowstone, grabbing a sapling for support.

Winkle's *Sultan* steamed past at a good clip, bows raising foamy waves, her two big low-pressure engines sounding boastful—*ssoooo—hah! ssoooo—hah!*—so different from Rosie's noisy exhaust. But they had apparently not seen *Rose of Dundee* hidden in the slough.

Someone stood on the hurricane deck, a tall figure in a plug hat, one hand holding it in place while coattails whipped about his skinny legs. That would be old Horace, searching for his kidnapped daughter. Beside him, spyglass to eye, was another man scanning the horizon; probably Julius Winkle. Forward, one of the crew stood by the three-inch brass cannon in the bows. If *Sultan* ever came in range of *Rose of Dundee*, Alec suspected that Julius Winkle would not hesitate to use the cannon.

Had the wood party heard *Sultan*? Alec looked over his shoulder, fearing that someone would run back, incautiously exposing themselves to the field of Winkle's spyglass. But they were too far away; the noise of the river masked sounds.

Cold and shivering, he stood in the bushes for a long time, watching *Sultan* steam by. Julius had probably not dared to run the Looking-Glass at night; he had laid to and come up in the morning.

If Alec had managed to stay ahead of her he might have

reached Fort Mahone and gotten the money Rollo Gamble promised. Then, when *Sultan* and old Horace appeared, he could have offered Nora's father the three hundred and fifty dollars he owed, and perhaps escaped prosecution for smashing the chain and defying the sheriff's writ. Now—

Soaked to the skin, he finally saw the great paddles from the stern aspect and watched *Sultan*'s wake flatten. For all that, she was a handsome vessel. In the rain he could no longer hear her engines. Well, Rosie was safe for a while, at least. But while Rosie lay in Potter's Slough, *Sultan* had gotten ahead of her. There was only one Yellowstone River; somewhere Alec would either have to pass *Sultan*, or admit he was whipped. Thinking of *Sultan*'s long bow gun, he shivered with more than the chill of the rain.

Chapter Eight

He did not think he was going to make it back to *Rose of Dundee,* for a moment experiencing a feeling of unreality that made him stop to wrap his arms about a tree. Trees seemed real, solid, comforting. Bone tired as he was, strung tight with responsibility, the shock of *Sultan*'s passing had shaken him. Finally, as he wagged his head like a spaniel to clear it, the real world came back. Alec left the nurturing tree and made his way to the boat.

The wood party was still sawing and chopping. Climbing over the gunwales, he shambled toward the nearest cabin and collapsed. In the final moment before he lapsed into something approaching a coma, he realized that the bed was Nora Tobin's. In a way it seemed highly immoral for him to lie in that virginal bower. But the bed was comfortable, and smelled nice. Most things that were immoral, he suspected, were comfortable and smelled nice. That was why they were immoral. On the edge of sleep, he realized why Nora had gotten into that immodest costume of jeans and shirt. Hanging from a line strung across the cabin was her washing; dresses, stockings, mysterious bits of lace, silk, and ruffles from which he modestly averted his eyes. Rosie—his own Rosie—was a working girl, and would not really be Rosie, decked out in frippery.

In a dream he soon imagined himself in darkest Africa. He and Nora Tobin had been captured by cannibals, as in the travel book that he had once read, *A Missionary in Africa,* by a Mrs. Griffith-Hawkes. He and Nora sat in a huge iron pot, under which a cheery fire was blazing. Around them crowded naked black men with nose-rings and long spears, jabbering in anticipation of a *ragout*. But Gamble—Lieutenant Rollo Gamble—stepped out of the luxuriant jungle growth and pointed his magical carbine at the savages. While they shrank back before his kingly presence, Rollo pulled Nora from the pot. Throwing her over his shoulder, he marched back into the jungle, leaving Alec for a cannibal stew.

"No!" he shouted, suddenly sitting bolt upright. "No!" he said again. "Damn it, no!"

Blinking to clear his brain of the terrible vision, he saw that he was not alone in Nora's cabin. Surrounding him were painted bodies, ribboned lances, amused faces striped with red and yellow and black.

"No!" he said again, but without real conviction.

The Sioux fell on him, pulling him from the bed and binding him hand and foot. Then they carried him to the forward deck, where he ignominiously joined the wood party. Dumping him among the other prisoners, they ran gleefully about, howling like banshees, stomping the deck in savage dance.

Hampered by the fact that Woolly Willie Yates's booted legs lay across his chest, Alec tried to count his companions.

"Uncle Hugh?"

"Aye. I'm over here."

"Frenchy?"

"*Sacre bleu*, Chinaman!" the woodhawk protested. "You knee in my gut!" To Alec he reported, "*Oui!* I here."

"Ben? Ben Bagley?" Then Alec remembered. Ben had gone ashore earlier in search of venison.

"They didn't get Ben," Rollo Gamble said morosely. "Goddamnit, why did I ever leave the practice of law? I had a woman try to cane me once in my office, and another lawyer challenged me to a duel, but there was nothing like this!"

Alec wriggled, moving to starboard like a snake trying to shed its skin. Finally he managed to inch his back up the gunwales and prop his head on the rail. "Where are the Chinamen, for God's sake?"

Sam Fat grunted. "In bilges! Run away, like mice! Crowards! All crowards! No guts!"

"The bastards come on us like a swarm of hornets," Willie snarled. "We'd stowed the last wood aboard, and was going back for some odds and ends when they jumped us." He spat, unsuccessfully, tobacco juice dribbling down his beard. "More the damned idjits, us, to cut wood without no lookouts posted!"

According to their practice the Sioux would have their fun—take anything shiny or useful, set fire to the boat, and watch the helpless prisoners fricassee. Well, Alec thought, perhaps the high-piled wood would make the fire hotter and quicker, putting them out of their misery the sooner.

"Nora?" He had forgotten Nora. Where was she?

Uncle Hugh, lying next to him, groaned. "Over there! Don't you see?"

Buffalo-tail fly switch poised like a scepter, Bad Eye himself stood by the forward capstan. He was a powerful bandy-legged man with a shaved scalp and a cruel mouth, savage in his tomato-can armlets. Nora Tobin, her wrists bound, stood before him, gaze haughty and defiant as the chief contemplated her, one orb filmed and the other obsidian-shiny with lust.

"You pretty," Bad Eye remarked, strolling appraisingly about her as she was held by a brave on each side. "You pretty like—" He groped among his English words. "Like flower." He chucked her under the chin. "Like white flower, you!"

The savages found what they were looking for—Uncle Hugh Munro's cache of Highland Elixir. Laughing and joking, they carried down kegs and placed them in a row. A pockmarked buck broke the head of a keg with his hatchet and scotch whisky splashed everywhere. "Great swith!" Uncle Hugh groaned. "Sacrilege!"

Rollo Gamble twisted in his bonds. "If that devil touches Nora, I'll—"

"Be still!" Alec muttered. "You can't do anything anyway!"

Bad Eye fanned himself with the buffalo tail. He said something, probably obscene, to Nora's captors. They laughed, and dug each other in the ribs.

"I'll kill him!" Rollo insisted. Rolling about, he finally managed to get to his knees.

"Like flower," Bad Eye said softly. He reached out, toyed with the taffy hair, rolling a silky strand about a finger. "You—me—bed." He jerked his head toward one of the cabins.

Furious, Rollo tottered to his feet. Like a jumping jack he hopped forward, protesting. One of the guards swung his rifle barrel like a club. Alec winced, thinking he heard ribs breaking. Rollo collapsed, moaning between clenched teeth.

Wresting free of her captors, Nora knelt beside him. "Oh, Rollo! What have they done to you?" Helplessly she raised her bound hands in supplication. "Sir, let me help him! He's hurt!"

The Sioux chief grinned down. "Bed!" he announced. "You—me!" He gestured toward a cabin and the guards, giggling, dragged Nora away, protests unavailing. She did manage to sink her teeth into the calf of one of the men, who howled and slapped her face.

"It didn't help," Alec muttered. "All Rollo got for his pains was broken bones! I'd have tried it myself except I knew it wouldn't be any good!"

"Eh?" Uncle Hugh asked. "What are you mumbling about?"

In a wild festival the savages capered about. Whooping, they splashed whisky on each other, dipped pannikins, coffee mugs, and cupped hands into the kegs, swilling it as if it were water. One man, staggering under the weight, lifted a whole keg to his mouth and gulped. Tipsy, he fell backward; the keg rolled about the deck, gushing whisky. The naked warriors played a game with it, yipping like coyotes.

"Good losh!" Uncle Hugh sobbed. "The work of six months destroyed! If there's a God in heaven the whole Sioux nation will burn for this day's sins!"

Without hope the prisoners watched the bacchanale. Willie, by steady maneuvering, managed to reach Rollo Gamble and drag him back to the group, safe from the prancing of Bad Eye's cutthroats. It might have occurred to them to make the lieutenant a part of the game with the rolling whisky keg.

"How do you feel?" Alec asked.

Gamble's pale face was beaded with sweat. "I think they broke something inside," he gasped. "I—I feel sick!"

Wilder and more exultant grew the dancing. Bad Eye himself joined the festivities, saving his rendezvous with Nora Tobin for the best and the last. He sat regally on an empty keg, fanning himself and drinking whisky from a battered tin pot, at times springing to his feet and prancing about the deck. Looking at the captives over the rim of the pot, the chief's eyes glinted with malice. *What new torture has he thought of now?* Alec wondered. It was his fault, all Alec Munro's fault. He was captain of *Rose of Dundee;* what happened to his people was his responsibility. But how was he to get them out of this predicament?

The sun soared high. In the heat the captives sweltered. Alec felt dizzy. He began to hear voices, strange voices. Above the cacophony of revelry the voices persisted.

"Alec! Can you hear me?"

The burden of what he had gone through had unhinged his mind. Spirits were speaking to him. He recalled his reading about the Fox sisters of Elmira, New York, and their insistence that spirits could communicate with the living. The sisters claimed, in a copyrighted article in the Bismarck newspaper, that there were spirit "guides" which came to the doomed and dying to prepare them for the journey to the other side.

"Alec!" The spirit's voice was insistent. "Damn it, can't you hear me?"

Suddenly Alec recognized the voice. It was his old friend Ben Bagley. Ben had been killed by the Sioux; now his spirit had returned to guide them all to eternal peace.

"Yes, Ben," he said soberly. "I hear you. What are we to do now?"

"There's hope, Alec. Listen—"

"I'm glad," Alec murmured. "I've been a great sinner, Ben —I'm ready to admit that now. I've done all sorts of things I shouldn't have. I should have treated poor old Uncle Hugh more kindly, and not called him names. I should have tried to get along better with Nora Tobin, and admitted I loved her. I shouldn't have been so rash and stiff-necked in this world. I ought to have kept in mind that a soft answer turneth away wrath and the meek shall inherit the earth. I forgot all these things, Ben, but now I'm glad to hear you say there's hope in the afterworld."

There was a pause. Then the voice asked, "What the hell are you talking about?"

The sheriff didn't sound like a spirit; he sounded more like an earthly Ben Bagley. Alec craned his neck. Over the gunwales he caught a glimpse of a whiskered face plastered with mud. It was Ben, clinging to the anchor chain, looking like King Neptune rising, seaweed-draped, from a watery kingdom.

Startled, Alec muttered, "I thought you were someone else!" He leaned back to be as close to the apparition as possible. "Have you got a knife?" he whispered. "If you can pass it to me, I'll cut our ropes and we can rush them."

"Not a chance! They're armed to the teeth, and working themselves into a state."

"But you said there was a chance!"

"There is! Just sit tight!"

Alec looked at the cabin where the braves had taken Nora. "Bad Eye threatened to—to—" His lips could not encompass the dreadful words.

"I know," Ben said, "but Bad Eye's getting drunk as the rest. Just sit tight, Alec, you and the others, and give them time. Ain't I had enough drunken Indians in my jail to know? They'll all pass out soon. Then I'll slip you my knife. By that time they'll be drunker 'n a skunk."

"But—"

"Listen to me, son!" Ben hissed. "You got a tendency at times to be a little flighty! Listen to an older man—one that's seen the elephant! Do what I say—hear?"

"All right," Alec whispered back. "I trust you, Ben! Always did!"

Some of the drunken red men brought wood from the stacks and piled it on deck. A Sioux with a buffalo skull tied to his crown shaved a billet into curls and lit a match. Flame licked at the dead wood; smoke curled. Alec swallowed hard. They were going to burn Rosie, along with her crew and passengers. Horrified, the prisoners watched.

"They're setting us on fire!" Alec cried.

One man, carrying an armload of wood, staggered and fell. Billets of bull pine rolled about the deck. Giggling, the brave bent to retrieve them, but fell. He tried to get up, but his legs would not support him. He lay flat on the deck, one hand shading his eyes from the sun, grinning vacantly. Another of the band slumped in Alec's old cane-bottomed chair. An empty tin cup dangled from his fingers, and he closed his eyes and started to snore. All about lolled the members of Bad Eye's gang. Some slept, others only stared glassy-eyed. One man, head on chest, talked drunkenly to himself, seeming to take both sides of a vigorous argument.

"Look!" Willie growled. "They're soused to the gills, all of 'em!"

Uncle Hugh spoke, sadly but not without pride. "That stuff was distilled three times. It had a nice bouquet, but it *was* powerful!"

The fire grew in intensity. Already the deck was charring. The coolies, smelling smoke, tried to climb out of the bilges, but Bad Eye had locked them in. They screamed, pounding on the heavy hatch cover till it clattered up and down, straining against the brass slide-bolts locking it in place.

Frantic, Alec worked his way upright against the gunwales to demand the knife from Ben Bagley. But Bad Eye, the only

Sioux still moderately sober, transfixed him with the milky-eyed stare. Alec shrank back when the chief clanked his armlets and drew a pistol from his belt.

"All right," he said hastily. "I was just stretching my legs!"

Rollo Gamble's groaning weakened; Alec feared that the lieutenant was dying. The Chinamen screamed, terror-struck at the thought of immolation. Shaken, Alec watched Bad Eye rise and start uncertainly for the cabin where Nora was imprisoned. The guards at the door had drunk their share of firewater, and more; they lay propped against the doorjamb, eyes glazed. When Bad Eye approached, one tried to rise, but collapsed. The other closed his eyes and snored.

"Ben!" Alec called in desperation. "Give me the knife, for God's sake!"

Reaching behind him, he felt the gold penknife that usually hung from the sheriff's watch chain. "Here!" Alec muttered to Hugh, rolling to one side. "Here's a knife! See if you can open it and cut the ropes on my wrists!"

Hugh was popeyed. "Wherever did you—"

"It's Ben Bagley's! He swam around to the port bow and passed it to me! Hurry!"

Bad Eye paused at Nora's door. He tried to turn the knob, but found it locked from within. He cursed a Sioux curse.

"That's who you were talking to, then!" Hugh exclaimed. "To tell the truth, I thought you'd popped your main steam line and gone crazy!" Sawing at the rawhide, his uncle cut flesh instead, but Alec hardly felt it.

"Hurry, damn it!"

Bad Eye raised a moccasined foot preparatory to kicking in the door. Unsteady, he teetered, falling against the doorjamb. Still cursing, he braced himself, poised for another kick.

Hands free, Alec cut the cords securing his ankles. Slashing his uncle's bonds, he cried, "Free the others!" and tottered up on legs that seemed to belong to someone else.

"Stop!" he called to Bad Eye.

Bad Eye kicked at the thin panels of the door. His foot

crashed through. The resultant splinters caught his bare leg like a shark's teeth, holding it immobile.

"Nora! I'm coming!" Alec staggered toward the door, but his legs doubled under him. It was Woolly Willie Yates who rescued Nora. Rushing forward, Willie grabbed the wrecked door and wrested it from its hinges. Carrying it high over his head with Bad Eye dangling from it, he threw the whole thing overboard into the water.

"Nora!" Alec cried. "Are you all right?" As blood started to flow in his cramped limbs, he started through the open doorway. But Nora Tobin rushed past him, weeping.

"Rollo!" she cried. "Oh, Rollo, where are you? What have the brutes done to you?"

Rebuffed, Alec leaned weakly against the doorframe. The scene on deck resembled the latter days of Sodom and Gomorrah illustrated by Mr. Gustave Doré in the Bible. Smoke veiled the vessel. Through the hole in the deck the faces of the imprisoned Chinese stared up, like sinners condemned to Hades. Woolly Willie Yates was busy chasing down frightened Sioux with a piece of doorjamb. Sam Fat swung wildly with his cleaver, shouting in Chinese. Frenchy Villard, spare frame given strength by anger, was busy throwing suddenly-sober Sioux into the water. Uncle Hugh Munro, a captured headdress on his bald pate, fractured Sioux skulls with a war-club studded with bear teeth. Ben Bagley, in nothing more than long underwear and dripping river grasses, was picking off stragglers with Gamble's carbine. He paused long enough to apologize to Alec.

"I ain't a very good swimmer so I had to take off my shirt and pants and shoes to swim around to Rosie's port bow. They're still on the bank somewheres, I guess."

The Sioux were finally driven off, the fire put out. A few of Bad Eye's braves gathered on the bank, out of range, and yammered curses, shaking their fists. It had been, Alec reflected, a long day. Dully he watched Woolly Willie bend over Rollo Gamble. Nora hovered near.

"I used to doctor horses when I lived in Macon, Georgia," Willie explained. "Horses' ribs ain't that much different from a man's." He spoke to Sam Fat, still carrying the bloodstained galley cleaver. "Have them Chinamen carry him gentle to yonder cabin and lay him easy on the bed. Miss Nora, you got any old dresses I could tear up and kind of stretch bandages round his middle to hold things in place?"

"Oh, of course!" Nora cried. "Yes, of course!"

It was Sunday; Alec insisted on a brief Presbyterian service of thanksgiving for their deliverance. Then they fired up and steamed into the Yellowstone, fearing Bad Eye and his people might attack again, appetites whetted by their monumental drunk. Alec, again at the wheel, looked down on a hole burned in the foredeck. Ben Bagley had rigged a makeshift line around the cavity with a scrawled warning on a piece of tin: BEWAR OF HOLE.

Attended by Nora Tobin, Rollo Gamble lay in bed with his broken arm and several newly fractured ribs. Frenchy Villard's wound had broken open during the fight with the Indians; Willie Yates, now ship's doctor, treated it with poultices of river mud and manure from Solomon Two and Pepperpot. Willie himself had lost most of his mop of frizzled hair, his eyebrows, and his beard fighting the fire. Ben Bagley, though he recovered Pepperpot from where he had tied her ashore on returning to find *Rose of Dundee* awash with Indians, never did find his pants and shoes, and no spare clothing would fit. In consequence he fastened a torn blanket about him, securing it with pins borrowed from Nora Tobin, and walked the deck in bare feet.

Hugh Munro had burned his hands fighting the fire and now could only superintend the stoking of the boiler and the maintenance of the engine. Sam Fat had lost the rest of his pigtail, a convenient handle for the marauding Sioux, and also hobbled about on a swollen ankle. The Chinese were serviceable, but still so frightened by the Indian raid that they tended to do little but chatter among themselves and watch the passing undergrowth with trepidation. Rosie, however, maltreated and knocked about as she had been, still performed like a thoroughbred. Some of her seams had opened, and Sam Fat routed out his crew at least once an hour to pump the bilges.

Alec did not speak of the passing of *Sultan* to anyone. That was his problem, to be dealt with when the time came. He would not worry the ship's company with any more troubles; they had had enough. He had an obligation to them—the weight of command, Rollo Gamble called it.

His uncle did not mind burned hands so much as the loss of several kegs of his Highland Elixir. "Six kegs, boyo—disappeared down the gullets of primitive savages! They could have been as well satisfied with bay rum!"

"Don't complain!" Alec said unsympathetically. "It saved our bacon, and there's plenty left they didn't have time to drink. Anyway, you could hardly call the stuff drinkable by civilized men! And it certainly wasn't aged, unless you want to call three or four weeks *aged!*"

Hugh wiped his nose, sighed. "Well, God be praised for what's left, anyway!"

"God never heard of you, you old heathen!" Alec sniffed, already forgetting his self-criticism when he thought he was going to pass over to the other side.

The Yellowstone fell no further, but stayed at an annoyingly shallow level. Time after time Rosie was forced to back and fill, steaming up one promising channel only to find it blocked by debris and sand. There was no recourse then but to back down and find another lead. Maybe, Alec thought, the river was too shoal for Rosie to reach Fort Mahone at all. But he was buoyed by one thought. *Sultan* was still ahead of him. Even unloaded, the bigger boat drew more water. Where *Sultan* went, Rosie could go and have water to spare under her keel. And if *Sultan* did reach Fort Mahone ahead of him, he would unload Rollo Gamble's cargo and accept whatever fate had in store. Actually, there was nothing else to do.

They came finally to the always-troublesome passage at La Boeuf's, where there had been in the old days a small French trading post. Even in decent water, passing La Boeuf's was a tortuous and demanding task. Now, looking ahead, Alec realized that they could not make it without sparring. *Sultan* had had to spar also, he noticed. Built for the deeper Upper Missouri, the bigger vessel had only recently left behind a great splintered spar stranded on the beach below the old cabin. In spite of the broken spar, Julius Winkle had managed to pass La Boeuf's. Alec was grudgingly beginning to respect the river skill of the master of *Sultan*. But then, a vessel as well founded, and with so much money behind her, could sail with spare spars. Alec could afford only a pair. One of those had been ruined when he let it fall on Rollo Gamble and his Sioux assailants.

"Give me five revolutions, uncle!" he shouted into the speaking tube. "We're coming up on La Boeuf's and have got to spar over!" Going out on the sagging hurricane deck, he yelled at Sam Fat. "Rouse up your boys and look to the spar! We're going to grasshopper over La Boeuf's!"

Sam Fat, little black skullcap gone and a tattered straw in place to hide the embarrassing loss of his pigtail, objected. "You crazy? Only one spar, Cap!"

Alec remembered one-legged Tim O'Blenness, who hopped around the saloons and card rooms of Springer's Landing on a single crutch.

"If Tim O'Blenness can do it, we can!"

"Everybody tired!" Sam Fat complained, but he beckoned to his men to unship the spar and lash it into place.

Word of the maneuver got to Rollo Gamble. Insisting on watching the maneuver, he persuaded Nora to have his cot carried on deck. Pale and battered, the lieutenant shaded his eyes from the sun with his good hand and watched. Nora stood at his side, fetching in a lacy dress festooned with green ribbons. Ben Bagley, standing beside Alec in makeshift toga, nodded approvingly.

"Miss Nora's a mighty pretty gal, ain't she?"

"Pretty is," Alec said succinctly, "as pretty does!" Through the broken window he yelled as Rosie slowed, scraping a bar. "Let her go, Sam Fat!"

The Chinese dug sandals into the deck and pushed hard at the capstan. The spar, one end deep in sand under Rosie and the other connected through pulleys and cable to the drum of the capstan, sank farther down as the slack was taken up.

"Give me half speed ahead, uncle!" Alec called.

Slowly the coolies wound the capstan, pushing and straining, skinny bodies almost parallel to the deck with effort. Rosie's paddles thrashed; she listed slowly to starboard as the butt of the spar found a purchase and the taut cable lifted her.

"A little more!" Alec called down to the engine room.

Rosie canted; for a moment the suction under her seemed to break. Then the same thing happened that Alec had often observed with Tim O'Blenness. Tipped on the starboard beam by the spar, Rosie swung sideways. Tim O'Blenness often went around in circles on his crutch when he was drunk.

"Damn!" Alec blurted. Tim looked funny, drunk, but there was nothing funny about *Rose of Dundee*'s predicament.

"We'll try again," he decided.

Again and again they performed the maneuver. Finally they scraped over the first bar, but there were others only a hundred yards ahead. Alec, sweating and irritable, kicked the binnacle in frustration.

"Wish I could help, son," Ben Bagley muttered.

Laboriously they crutched their way upriver. By late afternoon they still had not passed La Boeuf's. Nearing sundown, they seemed permanently stranded abeam of the old cabin. They were stuck, unless they could get a tow from some venturesome paddle-wheeler daring the Yellowstone so soon. The coolies tugged at the capstan handles until Alec feared the cable would snap or the spar break. Rosie heeled over, then slewed sideways again, yawing, but getting nowhere.

Frustrated, Alec mopped his brow. Though the river air was cool, he perspired.

"I know you're trying!" he wheedled, speaking to Rosie, "but we've *got* to get over this damned bar!"

Ben Bagley cleared his throat. "Looks like maybe we spend the night here."

"Or forever!" Alec was glum. Then a sudden inspiration hit him.

"Sam Fat!"

The straining coolies at the capstan slacked on the handles and squatted on the deck.

"Take a line from the forward port bitts and run it to that lone cottonwood on the far bank!"

Sam Fat blinked. "What you say?"

"You heard me!" Alec pointed. "Take your men and wade, swim—I don't care how you get there—but snub the line around that cottonwood. Pull—pull *hard*—when I give you three blasts on the whistle!"

"Swim? Chinamen no swim! That for fish!"

"You get over there and get there fast! It's getting dark, and we've maybe got one good chance left before we settle into the mud for good!"

"But dragons—"

Rollo Gamble's carbine was propped in a corner of the pilothouse. Alec seized it and squeezed the trigger. A splintered hole appeared in Rosie's deck planking near Sam Fat's black-slippered feet.

"All right!" he screamed. "I go! God damn!"

In the gloaming the Chinese splashed, floundered, and dog-paddled across the water, carrying the line. Alec called down to the watching group below.

"I hate to ask this of you, folks, but us white people are going to have to man the capstan now that the Chinamen are on shore. With the coolies pulling hard on the port line, and you all turning the capstan, there's a chance we can get Rosie out of this damned sand!"

Ben Bagley, toga flapping, hurried down the ladder. Frenchy, bad arm and all, grabbed a spoke of the capstan. Willie Yates leaned his bulk against the neighboring spoke. Rollo Gamble tried weakly to rise from his cot, but Nora pushed him back. Hiking up her petticoats, she ran to the capstan.

Alec called into the speaking tube. "Uncle, give her full ahead! Then run forward and lay to the capstan with the others!"

When the paddles started to splash, gradually picking up speed, he secured the wheel with the rope bridle and pulled the cord to loose an ear-shattering trio of blasts. Frightened, Pepperpot and Solomon Two neighed shrilly, and kicked out. Alec ran below to help.

"Push!" he yelled. "Goddamnit, push! Put your backs into it!" Gasping with effort, he put his head down like a mule, feeling his boots scrabble across the deck. "Push! Push!" In his desperation he slipped, skinning his knees, and scrambled up again. "Push!"

Rosie heeled; the starboard rail rose. Bubbles and black muck churned along her rail as the suction was loosened. Higher and higher she rose, then started the customary yaw. But the strain from the port line, with all the coolies pulling from the bank, wrenched her back. Like a compass needle, Rosie swung a little this way, a little that—uncertain.

Supplementing Alec's pleas, Ben Bagley joined in. "Push! All push!" Frenchy chimed in chorus. "Push, by damn!" Willie Yates, forehead beaded with sweat, growled, "Push! Break your damned backs!" Nora's soprano sweetened the growling chorus. "Push! Oh, push—do!"

Feeling his boots slipping out from under him again, Alec leaned on the long handle, unable to push anymore. But suddenly Rosie ceased her vague wanderings. There was a great whirlpool along the rail and a bubbling of foul gases. For a moment the vessel trembled, as if faced with a decision. Then she slipped free of the muck and ran straight ahead into deeper water.

Uncle Hugh dashed to the engine room to shut down the engine while the rest cheered, slumping at the capstan. Alec dragged himself up the ladder and leaned on the wheel. The long spar, duty done, bumped alongside Rosie. As they slowed, Alec shouted below. "Willie, will you please take the dinghy and pick up Sam Fat and his people? We'll lay to here till you shuttle them aboard."

Exhausted, he could only continue to lean on the stout oaken wheel and watch the sinking sun. In the narrow confines of the channel the trees and bushes lining the bank were aswarm with small black gnats that stung unmercifully. One day—was that what they had? Or two? He was unable even to raise a hand against the tormenting gnats.

Chapter Nine

The Yellowstone finally reached a state of stability, but at a level appropriate to August rather than June. Looking more like a scarecrow than a lightning pilot, Alec maneuvered *Rose of Dundee* carefully upstream. Lieutenant Rollo Gamble, confined to his litter below, called querulous messages to the pilothouse.

"How far now?"

Alec sighed, glanced at the chart. "Fifty—sixty miles yet!"

"We'll never make it on time!"

When Alec didn't answer, Gamble resumed his worries.

"I hear we're about out of wood! Going ashore to cut wood will take a good half day! Listen, I've got an idea! We can—"

Alec stuffed cotton waste in his ears. He was tired of Gamble's fumings. In addition, he was annoyed by the fact that they had not yet caught up with Winkle's big *Sultan*. Damn Winkle! Still ahead! Now they were passing more and more downriver traffic—mackinaws, bullboats piled high with furs, lumber rafts, quarterboats. He hailed one through his speaking trumpet.

"Seen Missouri Packet's *Sultan?*"

The man, a Frenchman manning the sweep on a barge, cupped a hand to his ear. "You boat make damn much noise, *monsieur!*"

"Have—you—seen—*Sultan?*"

"*Oui, capitaine!*" The lanky bearded man spat, jerked a thumb astern. "Up there! Fish Head!"

"Thanks," Alec said.

In addition to the shallow waters of the river, Alec had

other worries; the Chinese were becoming mutinous. Seeing them gather in small groups and chatter angrily among themselves, he asked Sam Fat, "What in hell's going on with your people?"

Sam Fat, spelling him at the wheel, was bland. "Do' know."

"You do too know!" Alec took a handful of Sam Fat's dirty blouse. "What's the trouble, eh?"

Sam Fat shrugged. "Unhappy, them!"

"I know they're unhappy! What are they unhappy about?"

"Tired eat nothing but fish! No pay, too—run out of opium for pipes—scared of Indians—hard work—all same make unhappy!"

It was true; Alec had long feared that their celestial patience would start to fray.

"Tell them when we get to Fort Mahone everything is going to be all right. I'll pay off the Tobin Marine Works debt, and there'll be plenty of downriver freight and passengers so I can give them their money. Maybe a bonus, too, for sticking it out so long."

Sam Fat shrugged, watching the river ahead. "I tell them! But do' know."

They were almost out of the wood they had cut at Potter's Slough. Soon they should land to cut wood again, but there was no time for that if they were to reach Fort Mahone by the twelfth. If Alec had money, it would be simple; stop at one of the woodhawk landings and take aboard twenty cords. But they had no money. Uncle Hugh collected only eight dollars and thirty cents from the passengers and crew. Wood—even spongy cottonwood—cost five dollars a cord.

"Most of that money was Ben Bagley's," Hugh reported. "He didn't hardly want to donate it—said it might look like aiding and abetting the flight of a fugitive—but he finally give in."

Alec looked at the pitiful handful. "Give it back to him," he instructed. "Give it back to them all, with my thanks."

There were more delays. The main steam line to the engine,

twisted and weakened by Rosie's groundings and the consequent warping of her hull, sprang a leak. They lost a full head of precious steam while they lay to at Fish Head Curve, repairing the long pipe. Uncle Hugh bent over the break, shaking his head. Woolly Willie Yates pushed him aside.

"Used to be a steam fitter in the roundhouse at Memphis, Tennessee," he remarked. Uncoupling the defective section with a spanner Uncle Hugh brought in his bandaged hands, he cut a sleeve from the galley stovepipe and slipped it over the rent in the steam line, binding it with lashings of cordage. Bolting the bad section in place again, Willie straightened, wiping sweat from his forehead. "Ain't pretty, but it'll maybe hold for a while!"

Uncle Hugh fired off the boiler again with some of the rapidly vanishing wood, supplemented with part of the hurricane deck. When steam was valved again into the main line a plume of vapor escaped. But when the pipe warmed the metal expanded so that the patch held.

"It'll do," Alec said grimly. "It's got to do!"

Rollo Gamble called Alec to the cabin where he lay, pale and languid. Baby, Nora's cat, crouched on a windowsill. Nora sat at the lieutenant's side, feeding him catfish broth. He winced as he tried to sit up. "His side hurts him so," Nora explained. "Now, Rollo—you just lie down again! Alec can talk to you lying down, you know!"

"About what?" Alec asked.

Rollo's voice had lost some of the army briskness. "I know, Alec," he said, "that you've been doing superhuman things to keep Rosie steaming upriver. But with all these delays it looks like we're not going to make it. Tomorrow is the twelfth of June. So I thought it might be best to call the whole thing off."

Alec bristled. "Call it off?"

"What I mean—have Frenchy take Sheriff Bagley's mare and ride the rest of the way to Fort Mahone. The weather's good now. The trail is dry."

"But—"

"Frenchy can tell General Terry the supplies are down-stream only fifty miles. Isn't that what you said?"

"I did, but I don't see—"

"The old man can send wagons to off-load the stuff and carry it up to the post."

"It won't get there by the twelfth!"

Gamble shrugged wanly. "Better late than never!"

Seeing his discomfort, Alec was gentle. "Rollo, we made a contract. I agreed to get your cargo to Fort Mahone by the twelfth and I mean to do it!"

"But—"

Carefully he put a hand on Gamble's shoulder. "You just lie there and let Miss Tobin take care of you till the post surgeon can have a look at your ribs and your arm." He looked at Nora; the blue eyes stared back at him, unfathomable. "She's a good nurse—Nora is good at ever so many things! Now I'll hear no more of giving up!"

Nora followed him outside, closing the door behind her.

"Alec, I understand there's some trouble about money for wood."

"That's right," he admitted.

"What will you do?"

He looked about at the battered *Rose of Dundee*.

"Burn everything except the hull, and a place to stand while I'm at the wheel!"

She fumbled in her reticule. "Pooh! You know you could never harm Rosie!" She handed him a sheaf of bills. "I told you I had money. Take it!"

Obstinate, he refused.

"Don't be stubborn! Take it!"

"Only as a loan, you understand! I'll pay you back quick as I can!"

"Don't worry about that! I only want to see Rollo's supplies get to Fort Mahone on time. There's a very good chance he may make captain if he's successful."

Alec looked at her a long time, chewing his lip, aware of his growth of mangy beard. She looked so fresh and clean, and it had been a long time since he washed. He shuffled to one side to be downwind of her.

"Nora, I've not told this to anyone, but it's time. Your father and Julius Winkle are ahead of us somewhere. *Sultan* passed us the day we stopped at Potter's Slough to cut wood. You were all in the trees, chopping, and didn't see her."

"A—ahead of us?"

He nodded.

"But you've got to reach Fort Mahone before they do! If we don't—" She flushed; one hand groped at her throat.

"If we don't," he said, "your pa will be waiting for you on the dock. He'll snatch you off and take you back to Springer's Landing to marry Julius Winkle."

"I know," she said dismally.

"And I'll go to jail and all sorts of things will happen. I'll lose Rosie; Horace will paint her up like a soiled dove and sail her under the Missouri Packet Lines flag."

"I'll never marry Julius Winkle! The whole thing was a mistake—something Father tried to force me into! I'm going to marry—" Breast heaving, she paused. A bit of the lace at her throat came away in her hand and she rolled it nervously into a ball.

"You're going to marry who?"

"Rollo Gamble!" Nora's gaze was defiant. "Alec, I've accepted Rollo's proposal! He's a dear sweet man, with ever so much to offer a girl. I wanted to tell you, but you looked so fierce, stalking about the boat and yelling at everyone, that I—well, I was scared!"

He had suspected that this was going to happen, yet the shock took away his breath. For a long moment he stood motionless, trying to recover his blasted thoughts.

"Alec, you're such a good friend, always have been." She touched his arm. "You're captain of a boat. Doesn't that mean you can marry people?"

Dumbly he looked at her.

"It's legal, isn't it? That way there's nothing Papa could do!"

He shook his head like a steer dazed by a blow from the slaughterhouse maul.

"Say you'll do it!" she insisted.

He was too stricken to vent his anger with words. Shaking his head, he shambled away and laboriously climbed the steps to the pilothouse. Sitting on his stool while Sam Fat had the wheel, he glowered at the wad of bills.

"You got money?" Sam Fat demanded. "Look! God damn, plenty money, Cap!"

Alec was tempted to throw the whole packet out the pilothouse window, but frugality restrained him.

"Money," he admitted. "Plenty money—" He counted. "This will buy us maybe twenty-five cords of good river oak."

Sam Fat warily touched a greenback. "Enough my people back pay?"

"No," Alec said. "Not enough for that. But tell them—"

"They damn mad, you bet! No pay, no work, they say!"

"Keep them happy as you can," Alec said morosely. "When we reach old man Kinnear's place at Brushy Point, go alongside that ratty landing of his. We'll buy our wood there."

Nora was going to marry Rollo Gamble! And she wanted Alec Munro to perform the ceremony! The irony of it!

Kinnear was his usual skinflint self; Alec had to remind the old man that last year he had taken him free of charge up to Doc Kimball at Turkey Flats when a fit of apoplexy felled him.

"It ain't like you, Alec, to be so hard on an old man!" Kinnear whined, rocking on the porch of his little cabin. "All I got in the world is this here woodyard! It don't pay me hardly nothing compared to the work I put in!"

"And all *I've* got in the world is Rosie!" Alec retorted. "Rosie's my pet, and she eats cordwood like a hound eats beef bones!"

Mrs. Kinnear, hands folded across a fat middle, spoke. "Rufus," she said, indicating a lean and mournful hound, "eats table scraps."

"And that's about what you've given me!" Alec protested. "Cottonwood that'll burn like paper! How about some of that prime oak piled over there?"

"Oak cuts hard!" Kinnear muttered. "I'd have to get ten dollars a cord for that there oak."

Alec finally wore him down and they loaded five cords of oak in addition to the cottonwood. Even so, they spent all Nora Tobin's money. Now they would have to make it to Fort Mahone on what was stacked on deck.

Above Brushy Point Alec felt a new sluggishness to Rosie's response. Even with good steerageway she seemed stodgy in the water, and listed slightly. He frowned, staring at the spirit level near the binnacle. She was listing two or three degrees. But Rosie, cargo properly balanced, should split the bubble at the zero mark. She was that kind of a vessel; trim, straight as an arrow, perfect in equilibrium.

"Sam Fat!" he called.

The Chinaman left the group of deckhands with whom he was deep in argument and ascended the ladder.

"My people say—"

"I don't care what they say!" Alec interrupted. "Go down in the bilges and see if we're taking on water!"

Sam Fat did not like the bilges. They were wet, slimy with marine growth, and dragons also lived there; small dragons, to be sure, not like the big river dragons, but dragons to be reckoned with.

"I send someone," he promised.

"Don't send anyone! Go yourself!"

Grumbling, Sam Fat went below to pry off a hatch cover. Carrying a lantern, he peered into the gaping black hole. Almost immediately he drew back. "Water!" he announced. "Lot water in there!"

"I thought so!" Leaning out the broken window, Alec

shouted down. "How long has it been since you pumped the bilges?"

"Do' know."

"Well, you damn better find out, and quick! Get that rascally crew of yours together and rig the pump!"

Sam Fat got to his feet. "No pay, no work! My people got be pay, like I tell you!"

Was it imagination, or did the spirit level show another degree or so of list? In her gallant journey upstream Rosie must have sprung a leak. With the many groundings, the grasshoppering, and the constant vibration of the engine her planks had probably sprung. There was nothing they could do about it now but pump, pump, pump! Alec took the pistol from the drawer and stuck it in the waistband of his pants. "Hugh!" he called into the speaking tube. "Come up here for a minute and take the wheel! I've got pressing business on the foredeck!"

With his uncle at the wheel he bounded down the ladder. Sam Fat stood defiantly, arms folded. The Chinamen crowded behind him, bare feet shuffling on the deck.

"Sam Fat," Alec asked, "did you ever hear of hell?"

Sam Fat paled, but held his ground. "No pay, no work! This free country—no slaves since Mr. Lincoln!"

"Hell," Alec explained, "is not a free country!"

Sam Fat's moon face wrinkled. "Do' know about hell!"

Alec warmed to his subject. Presbyterianism had some juicy things to say about hell.

"Do you know where you go when you die?" Afraid Sam Fat might confound him with a gem of Confucian thought, he hurried on. "You go to hell, that's where you go! And if you think there are dragons in the river at night—friend, you haven't *seen* any dragons till you arrive in hell!" He raised arms over his head in the manner of the Reverend Mr. Malcolm Glendower, late of the church at Carnoustie, near the mouth of Loch Tay. "In hell they've got dragons that fly through the air and have eyes in their bellies so they can look down and grab people! In hell they've got dragons with hides made out

of boiler-plate shingles! They breathe fire and smoke and cre-
mate sinners like a fly on a hot stove lid! In hell they've got
wet slimy dragons that come up out of privies and drag Chinamen in, screaming and fighting and kicking. But that's nothing
to those dragons, all that screaming and kicking, because it
just livens up the meal a little!"

Woolly Willie Yates, splicing a broken line, drew near, fas-
cinated. Ben Bagley stopped his whittling. Frenchy Villard's
eyes showed rapt attention. Nora Tobin emerged from the
cabin where Rollo Gamble lay; when he called to her, she
said, "In a minute, Rollo," and continued to watch. Gamble
himself, looking pale, finally hobbled from the cabin on a cane
the sheriff had whittled.

Sam Fat wiped a sweating brow. "My people—" he quavered.

"The peculiar thing about all this," Alec went on, "is that in
hell you're never dead. Down there a dragon can fry you to a
crisp and eat you like a piece of ham fat. But the way the
Devil laid out hell, you spring right up and have to go through
the whole thing with a new dragon!"

Though understanding little English, the deckhands were
impressed. Woolly Willie muttered behind his hand to Ben
Bagley. "I used to be a lay preacher in Clayton, Ohio. Had me
a little congregation there, and laid into 'em right good of a
Sunday. But I ain't *never* heard no preaching to come up to
this!"

Drawing the pistol, Alec stuck it into Sam Fat's plump middle. "Either you get those slant-eyed rascals busy at the pump,
or you're dragon-bait!"

Sam Fat trembled. He wrung his hands; his eyeballs rolled
whitely up.

"I can hear them now! Papa dragon, mama dragon, and all
the little dragons smacking their lips and drooling over a nice
fat Chinaman for supper!"

It was too much for Sam Fat. He screamed Cantonese

threats at his crew. They broke in panic, running to set up the pump.

"Alec?"

At the sound of Nora Tobin's voice he turned, aware she had been one of the group watching his bluff.

"I—I just wanted to say—"

Uncertain, he waited. She did not speak further, only looked at him with something very feminine in her eyes.

"Well?"

She hesitated, sighed, and turned away. Hugh Munro scrambled down the ladder, saying, "You'd best take Rosie, boyo! There's ugly water ahead!" For a moment he hung on the rungs like a gray monkey. "Women," he remarked, "can stay in love sometimes with the damndest blockheadedest fools."

"What do you mean by that?"

"Nothing! Just a kind of philosophical remark!"

"I never knew you to be a student of philosophy, Hugh Munro!"

Hugh rubbed a stubbled chin. "There's book philosophy and there's people philosophy. It's an interesting philosophical situation when a young woman soon to be married to a good catch puddles up so quick."

Alec looked around, but Nora had retreated to her cabin. "I'll leave such things to the philosophers!" he snapped. "For now, I'm going to make Fort Mahone by the twelfth or go to hell in the trying!"

Hugh shook his head. "That isn't all that's going to hell around here!"

"Get back to the engine!" Alec ordered. "I'll need all the steam I can get for White Horse Bend."

With plenty of wood for the fires Rosie made the passage without difficulty. Beyond White Horse a perverse and clammy fog veiled the river. Alec, peering into the cottony stuff, made use of the whistle, listening as echoes caromed off bluffs or were swallowed by a stand of trees. Sometimes the blast returned in a faint and wavering voice—then he knew that the water ahead was clear, though some distance ahead another obstacle might loom. It was hard work. Sweat beaded his forehead and ran down his lean belly. Closing his eyes to hear better, he jumped as someone entered the pilothouse.

"That's a Goddamned noisy whistle!" Rollo Gamble grumbled. "A man can hardly rest with all that racket!"

"Rollo! What in hell are you doing here? How did you get up the ladder?"

"Shame!"

"Eh?"

Gamble sank onto the stool, hooking the cane over a nail. "Shame propelled me! By God, I said, if Alec Munro, after all he's been through, is still up there in that pilothouse doing a job for me, then I'm going up and help! I can't do much, but I'm game to try. When we get to Fort Mahone—and I know we will, even if we don't get there by the twelfth—I'm going to be standing on my feet when we steam in! I'll not have General Terry see me flat on my back!" He grinned a lopsided grin. "Anyway, there were bed bugs!"

Alec went back to squinting into the mists, now made rich and coppery by the rays of sun. In a few moments Rosie glided clear of the fog.

"There's another thing," Rollo added. "Ah—Nora. Miss Tobin. I'm—well, I'm embarrassed in a way, at how things turned out. You've got to realize, Alec, I was, or *thought* I was, a natural bachelor. I played the field, enjoyed the game, liked to be around females. But I never once thought of marriage! Until—until—" He broke off. "Damn it all, are you listening?"

Alec looked straight ahead. "Yes."

"It's hard for me to talk about this," Rollo muttered, "so excuse me if I kind of ramble! But Cupid has plunked me right in the butt with his little arrow." Solemnly he raised his good hand. "I swear by St. George's *Cavalry Tactics* I never had designs on Miss Nora when I came aboard. 'Pretty,' I thought;

'charming.' It wasn't till she came aboard that the thing happened."

The river broadened, became more shoal. Between the stands of giant cottonwoods flanking the channel Rosie appeared headed for a watery witches' cavern, like the forest Hansel and Gretel once entered. The dark opening had an ominous look to it.

"I suppose," Rollo mused, "it happened to Miss Nora the same way, all of a sudden. But we're both damned serious about it. We're responsible adults, though I've got a few years on her. And she *is* an angel! Alec, I'd give my life for her!" He coughed, adjusted the sling on his broken arm. "It isn't easy for a hard-bitten yellow-leg like me to talk so, but I wanted you to know—"

"Look!" Alec blurted.

"Eh?"

The forbidding passage had opened out somewhat. Alec blinked at the array of lights that dispelled the gloom. Rollo Gamble looked too, and cried, "What the hell is that?"

In the dusk *Sultan* blazed with flares. She was stuck fast on a bar at one side of the narrow channel. Like monkeys, crewmen swarmed over her, running lines, toiling at the capstan in the light of torches while her big wheel thrashed.

"Alec!" Uncle Hugh's voice was shrill in the bell of the speaking tube. "Sam Fat says that's *Sultan* ahead!"

"I know!" Alec called back. "Throttle her down, uncle!"

Hugh's voice was incredulous. "Are you daft? For Christ's sake, old Winkle's stuck good! This is our chance to pass him!"

Sultan and Winkle *were* stuck good. Even in the dim light Alec could see that *Sultan* sagged deep bow and stern, her midships high on the hidden bar.

"Five revolutions!" Alec said.

"But—"

"Quick!"

As Rosie slowed, the popping of her exhaust quieted. Alec

could hear shouts and cries from aboard the imperiled *Sultan*. Focusing the spyglass, he saw Julius Winkle standing on the hurricane deck, bellowing orders through his speaking trumpet. *Sultan* was mortally hurt; Alec heard escaping steam and saw crewmen running about in clouds of vapor as *Sultan*'s steam pipes leaked their contents. Both hog chains had broken, and *Sultan* sagged like a stale pancake.

"Serves them right!" Gamble gloated. "That'll teach them to refuse a patriotic duty to carry U.S. Army supplies where they're needed!"

Alec turned the wheel a few spokes to port.

"Where the hell are you going?" Gamble demanded.

"Alongside *Sultan*."

Gamble left his stool, hobbled forward. "I don't understand!"

"*Sultan*," Alec said through tight lips, "is a steamboat. I've loved steamboats all my life, ever since I watched the old *Carnoustie Maid* steaming down Loch Tay to Dundee. Even if it's Winkle's boat, I can't leave her here to break her back!"

Gamble seized his arm. "You're crazy! They'll clap you in irons and take you back to Ben Bagley's jail! Not only that, they'll take Miss Nora with them!"

Alec pushed him away. "I'm captain of this boat!"

"You're crazy, that's what you are! All else aside, what about my cargo for Fort Mahone? Do you realize tomorrow is the twelfth of June? Now that we've got a fighting chance to make it, are you going to throw it away to help Tobin and Winkle and their damned *Sultan?*"

Slowly Rosie crept toward the stranded paddle-wheeler. From below decks voices shouted up at Alec. "Damn—what you do, eh?" "Alec, that's *Sultan!*" "For God's sake, nephew, come to your senses!" In the welter of sounds Alec thought he heard Nora Tobin's clear soprano. "Alec—don't!" Aboard *Sultan* the frantic scurrying about, the cries and shouts, slackened. Men stopped in their tracks, watching *Rose of Dundee*'s approach.

"I'm going to throw them a line," Alec said, "and try to pull them off!"

"I can't allow that!" Gamble cried.

Torn with emotion, Alec bit his lip. What he was about to do was against all common sense. But steamboats were almost people. Steamboats were his friends. He could no more leave *Sultan* in danger of destruction than he could refuse to answer a call for help from a man going down for the third time in a maelstrom.

"Eh?" He turned at the jab in his back.

Rollo Gamble, bracing himself against the bulkhead, held his carbine out, brandishing it like a pistol.

"Sheer off! Alec, I'm not joking! Sheer off, I tell you!"

Chapter Ten

With engine throttled back *Rose of Dundee* drifted nearer and nearer the stranded *Sultan*. Old Horace was standing on the hurricane deck of the Missouri Packet Lines flagship, leaning on a furled umbrella and looking impatient. Captain Julius Winkle stood beside him, glum and silent in the torch-lit gloaming.

"Ben!" Horace yelled, catching sight of the sheriff. "Ben Bagley! What the hell you doing on Alec Munro's boat in that getup?"

Sheriff Bagley yelled back through cupped hands. "Uh—I been meaning to talk to you about that, Horace. Y'see—"

"I hope you got that thieving Munro in irons, Ben! And where's my little gal he kidnapped?"

Rollo Gamble pushed harder with the muzzle of the carbine; Alec winced.

"I kind of want to talk to you about that, too!" Ben called back.

They were closing fast. Now only about fifty feet separated the two vessels.

"Rollo," Alec urged, "put up that damned thing! You can't shoot your way out of this, you know! Sometimes the Army has to give over to the navy. Right now I'm the admiral, and I'm going to try a little diplomacy. It can't hurt my case if we stop for a few minutes to pull *Sultan* off that bar! Anyone can see she's in danger!"

"You can't do it in a few minutes! Anyway—"

Alec wrenched the carbine from Gamble's feeble grasp.

"I'm commanding here, and what I say goes! You're lucky I don't shoot you for mutiny with your own carbine!"

Rollo's face was pale in the glow of torches from *Sultan*'s deck. "My cargo—"

"I promised I'd get it to Fort Mahone by the twelfth! Whatever else I may or may not be, I'm a man of my word! So sit your butt down on that stool and keep out of the navy's business!" Through his speaking trumpet Alec called to Captain Winkle. "Stand by to take a line! We're going to pull you off!"

Horace goggled in disbelief. "Is that you, Munro?" Julius Winkle scowled, and there was a brief and bitter conversation between the two. Finally Winkle picked up his own trumpet.

"All right, Munro! Come ahead!"

Uncle Hugh's voice sounded from the speaking tube. "Alec, looks like Winkle's got a man standing by that Long Tom in *Sultan*'s bows!"

"I know. I'm keeping an eye on him. But Rosie's their only hope!"

Willie rowed the dinghy while Sam Fat carried *Rose of Dundee*'s only good hawser over to *Sultan*. *Sultan*'s crew wrapped it around the bitts while the dinghy returned.

"Give me a few revolutions, uncle!" Alec called. "Just enough to take up the slack!"

Dripping, the hawser rose from the muddy waters of the Yellowstone. It tightened; a strand of river grass, draping from the line, flew into the air from the tension.

"All ahead slow!" Alec ordered. To Winkle he shouted, "Hook her up, Captain! Give your vessel all the steam you've got!"

Rosie's exhaust began to pound. Her paddles labored with their *chung chung chung*. Astern of Rosie the water boiled while *Sultan*'s two big low-pressure engines sounded their own hissing and sighing.

"Full ahead!" Alec yelled into the speaking tube.

Sparks and cinders flew from *Sultan*'s tall stacks. Acrid smoke enveloped *Rose of Dundee*. Rosie's exhaust rose to an ear-splitting crescendo and Rollo Gamble put his hands over his ears. Burning embers littered Rosie's decks. From below Alec heard Cantonese curses as a coal must have burned its way through a quilted cotton jacket.

Alec leaned out the window. "Willie, warn everyone on deck to stand clear of the hawser! If it breaks it'll slice someone in half like a sausage!" Through the speaking tube he yelled again. "Is that all you've got, Hugh?"

Suddenly Rosie lurched. For a split second the hawser slacked, then tightened with a jar.

"She's coming!" Alec cried.

Again the hawser thrummed with tension. Rosie stopped dead in her tracks, paddles still churning. Alec pounded on the wheel. "Come on, old girl! Show *Sultan* who's queen of the Yellowstone!" Looking over his shoulder, he saw *Sultan* grudgingly begin her slide off the bar. Julius Winkle was at the wheel of the flagship. Alec could see the gleam of the pilot-house lamp on Winkle's gold-braided cap.

"Go it!" Alec shouted. "Go it, sweetheart!"

From *Sultan*'s deck came a cheer as the big vessel slithered free. "You've done it!" Gamble shouted. "Look—she's come clear! Now let's get out of here before they try to play any tricks!"

Sultan had indeed come clear. Alec wiped his brow with a tattered sleeve. "Yes," he agreed, "she's—she's—"

He stared at *Sultan*. Paddles still churning, she came on—and on.

"What in hell's the matter with him?" Alec demanded, watching *Sultan*'s bows cleave the water, seeing her huge superstructure loom larger and larger. He ran to the window, cupping his hands.

"Ahoy, *Sultan!* Shut her down!"

From below he heard Frenchy Villard's shrill voice. *"Au large! Au large! Mon dieu—everybody run!"*

Unbelieving, Alec watched the big vessel close on Rosie's quarter, paddles threshing, a bone in her teeth.

"They're going to run us down!" Gamble cried.

Rosie had lost way as her engine was throttled down, and lay almost dead in the water. *Sultan*'s bow, Alec calculated, would strike *Rose of Dundee* a little forward of midships, near the pilothouse. Rollo Gamble tugged at his arm. "Let's get out of here!"

With glazed eyes Alec waited for the impact. Mechanically he reached for the whistle cord, blew a long and lingering blast, knowing it would do no good. Rosie's shiny brass whistle was still sounding when *Sultan* plowed into her waist. Like a knife the iron-sheathed bows crushed gunwales, tore up planking. Rosie shuddered from the blow, reeled. Pushed sidewise in the water, she began to list.

Alec tried to cry out, but no sound would come. It hardly mattered now. *Sultan* was backing free, but Rosie was hurt, perhaps mortally. Dazedly he looked around, wiping his mouth with the back of a hand.

Rollo Gamble clung to the rail of the sagging boiler deck. He was yelling a warning, but Alec didn't understand. "Eh?" he asked.

Rollo pointed skyward. The remaining spar, the one they had used in the awkward one-legged grasshoppering of La Boeuf's, had broken loose and was tottering. Putting his hands over his head, Alec scrambled out of the pilothouse. But as he crossed the doorway the great spar fell, crushing the roof. He went sprawling in a thicket of broken planks, splinters, and tin roofing.

"Alec!" Gamble shouted. To someone below he added, "Alec's in there!"

There was pain in Alec's ankle. Blood dripped into his eyes. He hoped his head was not injured; he had had enough of that damned brown paper and vinegar. Wheezing in the dust, he staggered to his feet, wincing when he put weight on the right one. Managing to pull himself upright, he saw the pilothouse lamp lying on the chart table, glass broken. As the coal oil seeped out his charts of the Yellowstone began to smoke. Their edges curled, blackened, burst into flame.

"Alec?" Gamble called, stumbling through the wreckage. "Are you all right? Answer me!"

The great spar had broken in half; the splintered ends slid off the wrecked pilothouse and floated alongside. Ben Bagley's face peered through the wreckage. "Alec! Son, are you hurt?"

"I'm all right," Alec gasped, beating out the flames, "but I'm damned mad! That maniac tried to wreck us!" He tottered to the speaking tube. The brass bell was bent out of shape, but his shouts finally got an answer.

"Full ahead, uncle!" he cried. "We've got to get out of here!" To the sheriff he said, "Ben, hurry aft and cut the hawser, if it's not already broken!"

"But you—"

"Hurry!"

Rosie's engine began, miraculously, to pound. Crippled, she slewed sideways while Alec fought to keep her in her marks. Frenchy Villard and Willie Yates climbed into the pilothouse.

"*Sacre bleu!*" Frenchy cried. "That Winkle! Why he do that?" Willie Yates grasped Alec's arm, asking, "You all right?"

"My ankle, I guess."

"You got a cut on your forehead looks like old Bad Eye himself done a job on you!"

Alec glanced over his shoulder. *Sultan*'s lights were falling behind as Rosie limped away from the scene of the crash. With the roof gone it was cold in the pilothouse. Overhead, stars twinkled, but there was no moon. He peered into the blackness. Where were they going?

"I shouldn't have risked you," he told Rosie. "It wasn't fair."

Frenchy, trying to wrap a dirty rag around Alec's forehead, paused. "What you say?"

"Nothing," Alec muttered.

"You sure you all right? Hit on head, maybe mixed up?"

"No, I'm all right, I tell you!" God, how his ankle hurt! He hoped it wasn't broken.

"It's up to you, sweetheart." He spoke again to Rosie, ignoring Frenchy's puzzlement. "Show me the stuff you're made of. Tomorrow is the twelfth of June, and I gave my word!"

Sultan's lights glowed far astern. When they rounded the Hogback—Alec guessed it was the Hogback from the loom against the starlight—even those small smears of light were gone. Now they groped their way like Blind Gamage, the old man who played the fiddle in the Sporting Life saloon.

Below, someone had had the sense to light all the lanterns they could find and rig them on poles alongside. Gnats surrounded the feeble yellow glow, but at times Alec could make out the ghostly trunks of trees on shore sliding past them and steer accordingly. Soon he was aware of other presences climbing through the wreckage, other voices. Sam Fat pushed him aside and took the wheel. "You tell me where go, Cap. Sit down, rest feet."

Alec slumped on the stool. His ankle throbbed. Cautiously he pulled up his jeans to look.

"Ain't busted, I don't think," Willie Yates said, holding a lantern near. He peeled Alec's boot off, gingerly flexing the ankle.

"Good God!" Alec gritted.

"Moves all right spite of the way it's swole already. Just keep your weight off till I can draw some hot water out of the boiler to soak it in."

"Alec," Rollo Gamble said, "Nora wants to know how you are." He peered at Alec. "You look like warmed-over death!"

"Maybe you ought to lay down for a while," Willie suggested.

Alec grimaced. "No one else knows the river like I do." He tried to grin. "You and me are a pair, Rollo—two bunged-up jokers! I guess when we get to Fort Mahone you'll have to lean on me and I'll have to lean on you!"

They swayed, reached for support, as Rosie slowed, ground on gravel, then ground free again.

"That was Alligator Shoal," Alec said. "I should have been watching! Now clear out, all of you! I've got a job to do!"

"Anyway," Rollo said, "your uncle sent this up for you." He held out a battered tin cup. "Says it'll give you strength."

It was some of the Highland Elixir. Alec, usually a teetotaler, shrugged. Anyway, the stuff would warm him against the chill. Someone handed him a blanket and he wrapped it about his shoulders, hunching forward to stare at the dark on Rosie's bows. It was the blackest black he had ever seen.

"Steady, now," he warned Sam Fat. "Steady as she goes!"

At times he must have slept, but woke with a start the moment Rosie betrayed by her least movement the possibility of trouble. On through the night they crept, the longest night Alec had ever spent. From time to time he raised the lantern to look at the clock, forgetting that the wall where it once hung had disappeared, and the clock with it. At times in their groping they brushed against trees on shore, and sleeping birds squawked plaintively and fluttered away.

Touching a hand to his forehead, Alec found the cut had scabbed over and was no longer bleeding. Too, the whisky somewhat deadened the pain in his ankle. Willie Yates had advised him to leave the boot off. Now he was glad he had done so, even though his foot felt like ice. The ankle had ballooned. By now the boot would have had to be cut off.

During the night they grounded again. Sam Fat called into the speaking tube. "Mo' revolution!" Sliding off, Rosie glided forward again into the blackness. Seeing Alec awake, Sam Fat gestured in protest. "God damn—hard keep her go straight!"

Alec remembered what a veteran pilot once said about the river: "Plays hide-and-seek with you one day, and the next follows you around like a puppy dog with a giant firecracker tied to its tail!" Right now the Yellowstone seemed more like a mastiff towing a fieldpiece. He knew that the mud bottom was laced with the bones of unlucky vessels.

"Let me take her for a while," he told Sam Fat.

Long delayed, dawn finally arrived. Now the Yellowstone looked like a Scottish lake, serene and untroubled. Ducks, pausing in northward flight, congregated in noisy flocks. Glassy waters reflected ribbons of pink and blue and gray, heralding the approach of dawn. In this idyllic scene *Rose of Dundee* looked like a floating junkyard. Both stacks were now only stumps. Rosie's decks were a jumble of scrap lumber, and she was stuck with arrows so that she resembled a porcupine. Still she bore proudly, if erratically, on, her wake spreading far astern in rippling nested V's.

"You're still my sweetheart!" he muttered. "There's no one can hold a candle to you!"

With the sun came activity below. Sam Fat put his men to pumping the bilges. While the collision with *Sultan* had done heavy damage to the superstructure, the only problem below the waterline seemed to be the loosening of some seams. Rollo Gamble hobbled through the wreckage to the pilothouse, assisted by Ben Bagley.

"Look here!" he said to Alec, spreading out a half-burned chart. "I make it no more than thirty miles now to Turkey Flats, and Fort Mahone is just beyond!"

Alec stared at the shoreline. The wide stretch in which Rosie now glided was called Tin Plate. "That's about right," he agreed. Rising from his stool, he almost collapsed at the needles of pain shooting like electric impulses through his damaged ankle. "My Lord!" he blurted, and sat quickly down.

"Knew it would be like that," Ben Bagley grunted. He held out a rude crutch, saddle padded with cloth. "I whittled it out last night. Miss Nora made a kind of a cushion from some padding from her—her—" He coughed, delicately. "From some of that stuff ladies wear on the back of their laps."

"I don't need that thing! I'll just—" Attempting to stand again, Alec turned pale, bit his lip. "All right," he conceded. "Didn't mean to sound ungrateful, Ben! Thanks—and thank Miss Tobin for me, too."

"Can we make it today, then?" Gamble insisted.

Looking at the lieutenant's broken arm and the bandaged ribs, the Kossuth hat sagging and the once imperial moustaches brushy and untrimmed, Alec forced a smile. "Maybe Rosie can," he grinned, "but I don't know whether *we* will unless we stop getting bunged up so!"

"I'm not joking! This is the twelfth of June! Can we make it today?"

"Possible."

"What do you mean, possible?"

"We've still got to pass through Laundry Chute, just below Turkey Flats."

"What the hell is Laundry Chute?"

"They call it that because it's generally full of foam and bubbles, like a washtub of a Monday. Rosie's got near half her paddle blades missing, and Hugh's engine is beginning to sound like an old mare with the wheezes. Rosie's limping along sideways, and water's coming into the bilges almost faster 'n it can be pumped out. With all that, we'll probably have to take the Chinese off the pumps and winch our way up Laundry Chute."

"But there's a chance?"

"Some chance."

"We're bound to make it, I know! After all that's happened, we're *bound* to make it! We—we—" Suddenly shamefaced, Rollo broke off. "Here I am shooting off my mouth about 'we this' and 'we that,' but it's not 'we' at all, is it? I mean it's *you*, Alec; Captain Munro! *You* did it! The rest of us, for various reasons, came along for the ride."

"Nonsense!" Alec flushed. "We *all* did it! Everybody helped! And Rosie did it most of all!"

In midmorning Alec, dozing on the stool while Sam Fat steered, was awakened by a fierce caterwauling and a torrent of Cantonese, broken off by the report of a gun.

"What the hell?" he demanded, sitting bolt upright.

Peering down on the wreckage of the main deck, Sam Fat frowned. "Do' know! Can't see nothing!"

Picking up his crutch, Alec half stumbled, half hopped through the broken timbers, sliding down the sagging hurricane deck. Rollo Gamble stood at bay on his cane, surrounded by angry Chinese.

"Back!" he roared. "Stand back, you heathen!"

Cats ran about the deck, slinking furtively into nooks and crannies, meowing piteously. Seeing Alec, Gamble gasped, "Get your pistol! It's an insurrection!"

Alec broke through the circle, brushing the coolies aside. "What's the matter here?"

Recognizing authority, the Chinese drew back. One man bowed deeply and started to jabber at Alec while the rest joined him in a kind of dirge.

"They're after my cats!" Gamble protested. "Back there, sir!" Neatly he booted a cat into a broken crate. "And stay there!" To Alec he said, "Miss Nora and I were just talking in the middle of the boat—"

"The waist!"

"Waist, then! Anyway, her cat—Baby—pricked up her ears and started to meow. Then we saw other cats strolling along the deck and I went to investigate." Rollo pointed. "These damned Chinamen were stealing cats—U. S. Government property, mind you—to *eat!*"

Alec had never liked cats. "I'd think you could spare them a few," he said mildly. "After all, the Chinese are getting hard to live with. They haven't been paid for months, and they're hungry, too."

Rollo shook his head. "There's a law against it!"

"A law against eating cats?"

"You know what I mean! I signed for those cats at Fort Van Buren, and I mean to deliver every last one of them dockside at Fort Mahone!"

Alec sighed; the bureaucratic mind! "Well, I'll have Sam Fat speak to his people and try to reason with them. But they're awful hungry, and so am I."

"Alec?"

He turned.

"Does—does your ankle hurt very much?" Nora asked.

Pain lanced his heart. She looked meltingly feminine in a fresh yellow dress with a starchy collar.

"No," he said gruffly. "Not very much. It'll be all right."

The pain in his ankle was as nothing compared to the wound in his bosom. Turning his back on her, he stumped away and spoke severely to Sam Fat about his inability to control the coolies.

While Sam Fat went below to conciliate his boys with a promise of rice and tea and back pay at Fort Mahone, Alec again took the wheel. Somehow or other, he thought with Scots caution, things were going too swimmingly. The river was too placid, the Chinese too easily mollified, the arduous journey too near its end. Slapping at the cloud of gnats that swarmed about his face, he listened to the sound of the pump as Sam Fat exhorted his janissaries to greater effort. *Does it hurt much, Alec? No, not very much!*

When they came up to Laundry Chute he knew that his misgivings had been justified. Perilous jags and needles of granite stuck up in the narrow channel and the current looked to be at least six knots. While he considered the situation Alec rang down the engine and nudged Rosie near the foam-flecked shore. Frenchy Villard stood at his shoulder, sucking his teeth.

"She go, Alec?"

"I don't know. Look at that water coming down!"

"Mon dieu—what we do now, eh?"

Rollo Gamble joined him in the shattered pilothouse, along with Willie Yates and Ben Bagley. "Looks like the old washerwoman's busy today," Willie grunted. "Never seen her like this!"

"We've got to warp up," Alec decided. "It's the only way we'll ever make it. Take a line above the shoals, bring it back through the capstan, all hands crank like mad—the way we did back at La Boeuf's."

"I hope you got another cable," Ben Bagley said. "I cut the one with the ax when *Sultan* rammed us."

Willie Yates cleared his throat. "I figured we might need another one," he said. "I found an old rotten hawser in a locker and spliced it together." He scratched his chin diffidently. "Used to be a deckhand on a ferryboat in Camden, New Jersey."

Alec picked up the speaking trumpet and hailed Sam Fat. Rollo Gamble spat over the side, looked gloomy. "How long will it take, then?"

Alec shrugged. "Depends."

"On what?"

"On the good Lord, mostly. All pray." He picked up the speaking trumpet again. "Where *is* that confounded Oriental?"

Frenchy peered over the side into the greenery. "See him not five minutes ago. He and his boys *parlent*—speak together." The woodhawk cupped his hands, yelled. *"Homme Chinois,* captain want you! Where in hell you?"

There was a muffled expletive from the mangled engine room speaking tube.

"That you, Hugh?" Alec asked, putting his ear near the brass bell.

His uncle swore. "Damned cylinder-head gasket's leaking like a sieve! I don't know how long I'll be able to hold this old coffee grinder together with stove bolts and baling wire!"

Willie Yates returned from a search of the main deck. "Ain't nary Chinaman in sight, nor Sam Fat neither! They're all gone—vanished into thin air!"

"That can't be!" Alec protested. "They were at the pump a minute ago, meek as lambs!"

"I don't know about no lambs, but the slant-eyed sons of bitches has disappeared!"

Alec yelled again into the trumpet. "Sam Fat, lay topside to the pilothouse!"

There was only silence, the lapping of water at the hull.

"There ain't actually no pilothouse anymore," Ben Bagley pointed out, "but he ought to get your meaning."

They swarmed below to look for the Chinese. Alec hobbled after them, cursing when he banged his foot against a timber.

"What ever is wrong?" Nora asked, scratching Baby's ears. "My goodness, what is everybody shouting about?"

"We can't find the Chinamen," someone reported.

She pointed to the dense stand of cottonwoods edging the shore. "Just a minute ago they all went off into the trees. I thought maybe someone told them to cut wood. They had tools with them."

Alec groaned. The mutinous Chinamen had probably run off! How were they going to warp up Laundry Chute with no strong backs at the capstan?

"We're not only missing a passel of Chinks," Willie Yates complained, "but the hawser I patched is gone!" He pointed. "When I come up the ladder, I left it laying right there by the hog chain." He swore, looked guiltily at Nora Tobin. "My knife's missing too—my good old Green River I had since I was a pup!"

They all turned to Alec.

"All right," he said. "Go ashore, all of you that can navigate. The rascals can't have gone too far! They're probably skulking in the weeds, waiting to be coaxed back, trying to plague us, that's all! Drag them back here, get them any way you can, but bring them aboard fast!" He looked at the afternoon sun, a brassy disk in an eye-hurting blue sky. "It's gone noon already!"

They scrambled ashore through the mud—Frenchy, Ben Bagley with his shotgun, Willie Yates, Rollo Gamble with the carbine in his good hand.

"Rollo!" Nora implored. "Come back here! You're not well! You can't—"

"I'll be a lot sicker if we don't find those Chinamen!" Pausing on the bank, the lieutenant looked back. For a moment he tottered, slipped in the mud, regaining his balance by hooking an arm around a cottonwood limb. "Wait for me!" he said, and blew her a kiss.

"Well!" Nora said with some asperity. She and Alec were alone on deck. "I declare! Men are such fools!" When she saw Alec standing nearby, she flounced indignantly away. "Baby," she told the cat, "we are all alone now! You must be my solace and comfort!"

"Damned cat!" Alec muttered.

The sun continued to decline. Alec could hear distant cries; once there was a gunshot. But in an hour the searchers returned, empty-handed.

"I guess they scattered," Rollo Gamble reported, gasping for breath. The lieutenant's hands and face were scratched by berry vines and wild roses. "I thought I saw that big fellow—the mean-looking one that was the ringleader in that plot to eat my cats—but when I fired my carbine he disappeared in some trees."

"Never caught sight of a single one," Willie Yates said.

Frenchy Villard nodded, ruefully. "How you say—no hide, no hair?"

"They're gone," Ben Bagley sighed. "Clear off the face of the earth!"

"They've *got* to come back!" Alec raged. "They're scared to death of Bad Eye and his people! Anyway, when it starts to get dark they'll probably come straggling home. No Chinaman wants to spend a night in the woods with all the dragons and monsters that live there!"

"By then," Rollo Gamble said moodily, "it'll be too late! The twelfth is fast disappearing." He looked at the declining sun.

Alec ground one fist into the other. What to do? He looked upstream, where the foaming riffles of Laundry Chute sparkled in the late sun. No—not a chance, without the Chinese!

"Wait a minute!" Willie growled.

They looked, following his pointing finger.

"There they go," he said.

A mile down the river a strange craft embarked. The make-shift raft, fallen logs lashed together with what must have been pieces chopped from the stolen hawser, was awash with black-clad Chinese.

"Well, I'll be Goddamned!" Alec muttered.

Gamble tugged fiercely at his moustache. "The black-guards!"

"I don't blame them. They're better off drifting downriver. They can probably pick up another boat soon—they all want Chinese deckhands because they work for less. Any other boat would pay better, I guess, and have better grub." Suddenly he paused, felt his stomach turn over. *Sultan,* off the bar and with repairs made, could be steaming up the river now, not far from where the Chinese were disappearing around a bend.

"I guess that's it, then," Gamble said somberly. He took Nora's hand and patted it. "I haven't been a sailor very long, but it don't look to me like you'll ever get this shambles of a boat up those rapids, Alec."

Alec was stung. "Put that guff where the monkey put the nuts, Rollo! All Rosie needs is a little maintenance!"

"You needn't talk that way in front of my intended! That was a coarse expression!"

Alec hooted. "I first *heard* it from Nora Tobin!" Limping on the crutch, he clambered through the wreckage to the blasted pilothouse. "Uncle Hugh!"

"Eh?"

"We're going up Laundry Chute!"

There was a pause. Alec heard the gurgle of a bottle.

"We're going up Laundry Chute! I'll need every pound of steam you can coax out of that old boiler! Two hundred and fifty pounds, at least!"

"Swith, the safety valve's set to pop at two hundred, Alec! And we'll blow up before we ever get *that* high!"

"Nevertheless! Get busy!"

"But we'll fly higher than the moon!"

"We're not headed for the moon!" Alec shouted back. "We're heading for Fort Mahone, Idaho Territory. By the Lord Harry, I'm going to get there before midnight of this day! Pile on the wood!"

Chapter Eleven

Quivering in every plank, the cannonading exhaust punctuated by steam as the safety valve popped, *Rose of Dundee* rushed at Laundry Chute. Alec, propped on his crutch in the ruined pilothouse, dragged the wheel this way and that to miss the rocks menacing Rosie's hull. Rollo Gamble, at his side, said, "You know what the hell you look like?"

"A scarecrow, I suppose!"

"No, the Flying Dutchman! He's a crazy sailor man in an opera, condemned forever to prowl the Seven Seas!"

Alec pulled hard at the wheel, cursing. "I never saw an opera," he said, "but there used to be a man with some trained dogs came to Carnoustie every summer when I was a boy in Scotland!"

"Look out!" Gamble yelled.

Alec spun the wheel the other way. "I saw it!"

Now they were two or three hundred yards into the boiling Chute. Rosie groaned with the effort. Paddles digging in so that a mist of water enveloped the boat, she gradually lost momentum from her initial run. Soon they were only holding their own against the current. Heavily loaded, Rosie's bows dipped low; sheets of water poured over the main deck.

"Steam!" Alec yelled into the mangled speaking tube. "Uncle, can you hear me?"

Hugh Munro's voice was faint against the din. "That's all I've got! The old engine's shaking on her bed-bolts, and the cylinder gasket's leaking! If she blows—" He left the sentence unfinished.

Gamble looked at the swirling waters. "What will we do? You can hardly back down!"

Alec wiped spattered mud from his face. "There's a kind of spire of rock sticking up there, beyond that tree that's lodged in the eddy." Snatching up his speaking trumpet, he motioned to Gamble to hold the wheel while he yelled over the side.

"Ben! Frenchy! I'm going alongside that skinny rock that sticks up over there! Throw a loop with the bow line to snag us before we lose way!"

Through the wreckage of the hurricane deck he could see a shadowy figure move forward in response to his order. But neither Ben nor Frenchy emerged into the sunlight.

"It's Sam Fat!" Gamble blurted. "Where the hell did *he* come from? I thought he went downriver on the raft with the rest of his people!"

Sam Fat, dirty and bedraggled, stood like a figurehead as *Rose of Dundee* inched up to the slender needle. Waves battered him, muddy foam covered his body, but he did not flinch. With a twist of his wrist he scaled the loop into the air; it settled neatly around the rocky spire. Alec heaved a sigh of relief as he rang down the engines to half speed and Rosie was stayed against the current.

"I don't know where the hell he's been," he gasped, "but I'm happy he's back!"

"Probably," Gamble guessed, "scared pure white from what you were going to do to him when you found out his Orientals ran off!"

Anxious faces peered through the frame of the pilothouse door. Ben Bagley was there, Frenchy in his dirty bandage, Willie Yates—Nora, too, looking frightened.

"Alec," she faltered, "what—what are we going to do now? Isn't it dangerous to stay here?"

"Dangerous to stay here, dangerous to go forward, dangerous to go back!"

Sam Fat's moon face hovered behind Nora.

"Where the hell have you been?" Alec demanded.

Sam Fat rolled his eyes. "Do' know!"

"You disappeared, deserted your post in a time of peril!"

Sam Fat trembled, averted his eyes. "Bilges! Stay in bilges! Scare of you, what you do when my people run away!"

"I thought so," Gamble said. "Well—"

"What we need," Alec muttered, "is more steam, a hell of a lot more steam!"

Uncle Hugh Munro, joining the crowd, shook his head. "Look!" He held out a spanner in his bandaged hand. "Look there how I tremble! I've not ever been so afrighted! It's like the anteroom of hell in that engine room, nephew! She's going to blow, that old engine! She's going to blow, and take us all to perdition!"

"*Much* more steam!" Alec said with heavy emphasis.

"But—"

"That's the only way we'll get out of this pickle! Every minute we hang here our situation's getting worse! Soon the old girl will just break apart and drop us all unshriven into the Yellowstone!"

Hugh's voice was sarcastic. "And how, Mr. Captain Munro, do you propose to get any more horsepower out of that old relic?"

"Tie the safety valve down and—"

"You're daft!" Hugh's whiskered face turned ashen. "That's against all reason! Didn't you hear her popping away as it is? That safety valve is set to open about three blessed ounces before the boiler explodes!"

"Tie the safety valve down and pour scotch whisky on the fires!"

Hugh's eyes bulged. The disabling of the safety valve was bad enough. The wanton waste of scotch whisky was sheer madness. His voice cracked with disbelief.

"You're loony!"

"It's our only chance, uncle!"

Hugh retreated to the sagging rail where the remaining kegs were lashed. Striking a heroic pose, he flung out his arms as if protecting widows and orphans from a rapacious landlord. "You'll not touch a drop of my Highland Elixir! Why, it's mother's milk, it's nectar, ambrosia, it's *scotch whisky*, Alec!"

"Ben," Alec said remorselessly, "will you and Willie take those kegs below and stack them near the boiler?"

Sweaty gray curls stood up all over Hugh Munro's head. "Back!" he warned, brandishing his spanner. "Back, you barbarians! The stuff's just beginning to age! You'll not touch a drop! There must be other ways!"

Ben and Willie looked at Alec.

"No other way!" Alec confirmed.

As they approached, Hugh Munro adopted a combative stance. Willie Yates picked him up and set him to one side. "Little man," he warned, "don't get in the way! I ain't yet forgot that trick ring of yours with the mirror set into the bottom!"

"The rest of you," Alec ordered, "go into the bows! If the boiler blows that'll be the safest place—forward!"

Willie Yates, a keg under each postlike arm, said, "I'll stay with the old man in the engine room. He's that scared."

Frenchy, bowed under the weight of a single keg, balanced it precariously. "Me too, I stay with Hugh. He *ami, copain*—old friend. If I go to hell, I go in good company, eh? *Vive la compagnie!*"

When the rest left, Gamble cleared his throat, coughed. "If you don't mind, Alec, I'd like to stay with you. You know, get a good view of whatever's going to happen!"

Rosie's exhaust started to pop again, this time with an unbelievable din. Smoke poured from the stubs of stacks and flaming brands shot like projectiles into the air. Her hull shuddered as the paddles gathered speed, rotating in a muddy blur. Sam Fat cast off the bow line. For a moment Rosie hesitated, hung motionless in the current. Then she gathered her haunches under her and inched forward.

"Go it!" Alec shouted, pounding on the scarred rim of the

wheel. "Go it, old girl! Go it, you sweetheart! You can do it, I know you can!"

Rollo Gamble steadied himself against a post as Rosie's structures vibrated like a fiddle string. "Charge!" he shouted, waving his cane in the air. "By George, 'Into the valley of death'—how does that poem go?"

Heedless of rocks, Rosie picked up speed as she ran Laundry Chute. One of her remaining paddle blades broke free and flew high into the air. Gamble called out a warning. He and Alec cowered as it whizzed past and fell with a thunk among the wilderness of broken deck planking.

"Scots," Alec screeched, "wha' hae wi' Wallace bled—"

Clouds of white smoke from the stacks enveloped him; he smelled alcohol.

"—Scots, wham Bruce has often led—"

Rosie ground frighteningly on a rock.

"Welcome to your gorie bed—"

She spurned the rock, labored on.

"—or to victory!"

They reached the top of the Chute. For a moment Rosie hesitated, hanging on the foamy crest that lipped the placid basin beyond. Then she slid over, dug her bows deep, and started to clatter across the sun-dappled waters of Kelly's Pool.

"Unhook her!" Alec yelled into the speaking tube.

The din subsided. Rosie glided across the still waters, bow making little ripples as she lost way. Alec took a deep breath, swallowed. His voice was shaky.

"I don't know who wrote about the valley of death," he said, "but it was Burns I was depending on—Robert Burns, from Alloway, in Ayrshire, near old Mount Oliphant."

The other passengers flocked to the pilothouse, laughing and relieved. Ben Bagley clapped Alec on the back. Frenchy found English too restricting and babbled in French. Willie Yates half carried Hugh Munro topside.

"The old man can't walk very well," he reported. "His legs done sprung a spoke or something, and he's kind of glassy-eyed. But he done real well spite of that rattly old engine spitting steam at him!"

Hugh mopped his forehead. "Alec," he quavered, "don't *ever* do that again! Promise?"

"It was Rosie did it," Alec said, patting the wheel. "Sore hurt as she is, she came through like a thoroughbred jumper! Well—" He stood up, painfully, propped on the crutch. "We'd best be getting underway again!"

Hugh licked his lips. "I need a little nip, Alec! My gizzard is up amongst my tonsils someplace. Maybe there's a drop or two left in one of the kegs."

"Hurry it up! That damned Winkle and his *Sultan* could be down below, at the bottom of the Chute, right now! We can't let him catch us, we're that near Turkey Flats. Fort Mahone is not too far beyond!"

Gamble looked askance. "You mean Winkle can bring that big boat up this far?"

Alec nodded. "Howevermuch a rascal that man is, he's a pilot, I have to give him that! If they had spare hog chains, they'll be along. *Sultan*'s a bigger boat by far, and draws more water, but she's got two huge engines to our little one and she's running unloaded. Yes, I daresay old Winkle's cracking on all the steam he's got to catch us."

Beyond Kelly's Pool the river narrowed again. Still, it was a good two fathoms in depth, with plenty of room for Rosie and her thirty inches of draft. The sun was descending in the western sky when Gamble tugged at Alec's sleeve.

"Look!"

Alec looked. On a brush-covered bar extending from the wooded shore a lone horseman sat his mount easily, staring at them.

"That's a cavalryman!" Gamble shouted. "Other people don't sit a horse like that!" He snatched up Alec's spyglass and focused it. "Yes, by damn—Seventh Cavalry! I can see the number on the skirt of the saddle!" Taking off his hat, he waved it wildly. "On shore, there! Can you hear me?"

The cavalryman cupped his hands. "What vessel is that?"

"Rose of Dundee, out of Springer's Landing, with supplies for General Terry!"

"You Lootenant Gamble?"

Rose of Dundee was passing the lone rider.

"Yes! Our wagons got stuck in the mud so I chartered this boat to bring the stuff upriver!"

The cavalryman cupped a hand to his ear.

"I said—"

The rider shook his head. He rode his horse into the shallow water, gesturing.

"Can't hear you over the exhaust," Alec said. "Don't make any difference, though. The general will be expecting you now."

Gamble watched the rider, now astern, ride into the brush. "He's on his way to let Terry know we're coming. There'll be plenty of hands dockside to help unload." Leaning heavily on his cane, he sagged onto the stool. "I guess we're going to make it at last! After all these—"

"There's something wrong," Alec blurted.

"Eh?"

"There's something wrong with Rosie!"

"What do you mean?"

"I'm not sure! She just doesn't—she just doesn't feel right! After *Sultan* hit us, she started to yaw to starboard; I'm used to that. But now she handles real odd!" He peered forward. "Look how she's down at the bows!"

Rosie's prow dipped sluggishly into the river and did not seem anxious to emerge.

"Sam Fat!" Alec howled.

The Chinaman's head stuck up through a tangled maze of wreckage.

"Take another look at the bilges!"

Sam Fat bobbed his head, scuttled back into the splintered planks and timbers. A moment later he returned, sticking his black-capped head up through the wreckage like a gopher. "Water! Oh, damn—lot water!"

Cursing, Alec turned the wheel over to Rollo Gamble. "Can you hold her steady for a few minutes? There's nothing ahead but a straight stretch. Keep clear of that bar with the scraggly cottonwood on it!"

He crutched below, where Sam Fat had the hatch cover off. Not far under the level of the deck planking swirled muddy water. "You, Willie Yates," Alec said, "and Ben Bagley—get the bilge pump, quick!"

They ran aft to fetch the big two-handled pump, powered like a railway handcar. Frenchy Villard peered into the hole and said, *"Mon dieu!* How she float, eh, with all that water in her belly?"

Even as Alec was staring into the bilges the level seemed to rise. Water now splashed onto Rosie's decks, leaving a dark stain. "Hurry!" he called.

Willie and Ben came back, pushing and pulling the heavy pump with its crossbar handles. Alec grabbed the canvas hose and threw it into the bilges. Ben and Willie grasped the handles and started to pump. Although they were both big men, they could move the long handles only slowly; a meager stream of water trickled over the side.

"Me, I pump too!" Frenchy declared, grasping the handle. In spite of his injured arm he hung doggedly to the handle, going up into the air as the handle rose, banging his knees on the deck as it came down. Sam Fat joined him on the other side. Alec shook his head despairingly. What they needed was the vanished Chinamen.

"I'll help!" Nora volunteered. She put down the cat, Baby, and took the handle beside Frenchy Villard. "All together, now—pull!"

The trickle grew, became a fairly respectable stream, but there was a lot of water in the bilges. *Rose of Dundee* was still several miles from Fort Mahone.

"Are we getting anywhere, Alec?" Ben Bagley puffed.

"You're doing fine!" Alec lied. "If you can keep it up for a while we'll make it!"

How long could they keep it up—an old man, a wounded woodhawk, a woman, a wornout Chinaman, and Willie Yates? Woolly Willie was the only one with any real heft to him.

Painfully Alec made his way to the pilothouse. Rollo Gamble, sweating, turned the wheel back. "I'd not make a good pilot," he said. "It's too responsible a job, feeling all that boat under you and knowing you can run her aground any minute!" Mopping his brow, he asked, "Is everything all right?"

Alec shrugged. "They're all at the pump, working like mad." He scanned the half-burned chart, looked at the shoreline. "Turkey Flats should be around that next bend. Then Fort Mahone is only another three miles."

He searched for the scattered buildings of Turkey Flats, pulling Rosie along with the intensity of his stare. Holding the wheel with one hand, he leaned out the window. The crew at the pumps was still hard at work, though much of the starch seemed to have gone out of them. Still Rosie forged ahead, though now he had to allow far in advance for any change in direction; the vessel responded slowly, like a wounded animal.

"Keep it up!" he shouted to the pumpers. "You folks are doing just great! I can almost see—I can almost—" Looking upriver, he did indeed note a few scattered shacks along the muddy bank. "There's Turkey Flats! Only another three miles! Don't give up!"

After an epic voyage, *Rose of Dundee* limped into Fort Mahone at 7:37 P.M. on the twelfth of June, 1876. Nosing her carefully alongside the pier, Alec called into the speaking tube, "Uncle Hugh, done with engines!"

Rollo Gamble whooped with joy. "You did it! Goddamnit, Alec, you did it!"

"*She* did it," Alec muttered, patting the wheel. He put his cheek against the oaken rim and felt a kind of warmth return. "Rosie did it!"

General Terry himself rode down to the landing on a chestnut mare, surrounded by aides. He was a sad-eyed, long-legged man with a mattress of beard. In the slanting light of a June evening he looked with amazement at the stern-wheeler *Rose of Dundee,* out of Springer's Landing. Both stacks were gone and her decks were littered with wreckage. A huge hole was burned in the foredeck. The superstructure was stuck with arrows; many blades were missing from her paddle wheel, and the pilothouse was gone. Aft were lashed the box and wheels of a buggy; nearby a horse and a mule munched grass. A motley crew of passengers, including one woman and a man wrapped in what appeared to be a Roman toga, worked the bilge pump. Over all lay mud, wood ashes, and soot.

Coming aboard, the general looked around. "My God!" he remarked.

Rollo Gamble, arm in a sling, broken ribs bandaged, and dress blues in rags, saluted.

"Sir, the supplies you requested from Fort Van Buren have arrived at the appointed time."

"You're Lieutenant Gamble?"

"Yes, sir."

The general turned to Alec Munro.

"This is Captain Munro, sir, of the *Rose of Dundee.*"

General Terry stroked his beard, observing the crutch, the bandaged head, the torn clothing. "I—I don't believe I've ever seen anything quite like this, Lieutenant," he murmured. "I see you've brought Major Stockdale's cats, too."

"Yes, *sir!* I filled the requisition myself."

"General, could you have a detail of soldiers spell my people at the bilge pump?" Alec asked. "Some of my vessel's planking has opened, and she's taking on water. Tomorrow, perhaps, the Army can help pull her out so I can look at the hull."

"Of course, Captain! We have plenty of horseflesh. With some logs as rollers we can certainly accommodate you."

Relieved of their duties, the weary pumpers staggered

ashore and collapsed. Nora Tobin leaned heavily on Rollo Gamble's good arm.

"And who," General Terry inquired, "is this charming lady?"

"My fiancée, sir, Miss Nora Tobin. We are engaged to be wed. Ah—as soon as possible, that is. I hope your chaplain can marry us tomorrow."

The general nodded. "Of course, Lieutenant. We are moving out tomorrow to rendezvous with General Crook and Colonel Custer down on the Big Horn, but time can always be set aside for the holy rites of matrimony. And I hope you all will join me at supper tonight at Major Stockdale's quarters."

Nora was taken away by the post commandant's wife, Mrs. Stockdale. Rollo Gamble went to the bachelor officers' quarters. The rest stayed aboard, making their toilettes for the evening. Willie Yates unwillingly bathed in a tub filled with warm water drawn from the boiler. Frenchy Villard washed out a shirt and cleaned his fingernails. Ben Bagley borrowed pants and a pair of boots from a Third Infantry soldier. Sam Fat, embarrassed by lack of a proper pigtail, soaked a remnant of rope in dirty engine-oil until it was black and shiny, splicing it to the stub of his own queue. Uncle Hugh Munro, beard trimmed and wearing a celluloid collar, found Alec brooding in his cabin.

"Food!" he exulted, waving his bandaged hands. "Real food, nephew, after all that damned catfish! Even if it's army beef and beans it's going to taste like manna from heaven!"

Alec, head in hands, sat gloomily on the edge of his bunk, listening to the soughing of the pump as the army detail worked to keep Rosie afloat until the morrow. A swarm of soldiers had already off-loaded the cargo.

"I'm not hungry."

Hugh came closer, squinted in the rays of the oil lamp. "You're turning down the general's kind invitation? It isn't every day the lower classes get to sit at a general's table!"

"Nobody will miss me."

His uncle sat beside him. "Look here, boyo—"

"You've been drinking already!" Alec accused.

Hugh hiccuped, pressed a hand against his bosom. "Your father appreciated good whisky himself, once he came out of his stiff-necked ways! But how he ever sired such a blockhead as Alec Munro I'll never know!"

"Go away," Alec muttered, "and leave me!"

"I'll not! Listen to me, son of my brother! *In vino demitasse!* Don't you see she loves *you,* Alec?"

Alec laughed, hollowly.

"She always did, damn it! She still does! And she's pining for you to take her away from Rollo Gamble! Good losh, Gamble don't really love her! I've never seen a man that was more of a natural bachelor than Gamble! But he's dazzled by the lass, and thinks he's in love!" Hugh clutched him by the shoulder, exhaling inflammable fumes. "Save her, Alec! Save Nora Tobin from her own foolish pride, and yours! Don't let this thing go all agley because neither of you is humble enough to make the first move!"

"I can't do it, uncle! Nora made her decision. I'll not interfere at this late date. No, Rosie is my love! She's dependable and uncomplaining, which is a hell of a lot more than Nora Tobin is! Rosie and I will grow old together. Kismet, they call it, I think. Fate, destiny—whatever. A man can't fight it!"

Hugh stomped the deck. "Foosh, double foosh, and triple foosh! You're an idiot, a damned noodle-spined creature that doesn't deserve the proud heritage of the clan Munro!"

"Nevertheless—"

"But you'll come along to the general's table with us? After all, it would be an insult to his nibs if you turned him down!"

Alec rubbed a bristled chin. "Well, I guess I can do that much." He rose, leaning on the crutch. "I'm a sight to frighten children with! Have you got a clean shirt put by?"

The commandant's quarters were large and commodious and his cook was a good one. The general was gracious and kindly. Willie Yates ate his mock-turtle soup with too much relish, and Frenchy Villard wiped his hands on the hem of the tablecloth after a bout with partridge in wine sauce, but on the whole everyone behaved creditably. After a pie made of soda crackers but tasting remarkably like dried apples, the general rose, holding up his glass. A mess steward hurried to refill the goblets with homemade elderberry wine brewed by Mrs. Stockdale.

"I have a toast to propose!"

Dutifully the guests thumped their glasses on the table.

"To the happy couple, Lieutenant Gamble and Miss Nora Tobin!"

They drank.

"And to the valiant Captain Munro of the *Rose of Dundee!*"

They drank again. Some cheered while Alec kept his eyes on the damask cloth.

"Lieutenant Gamble," General Terry added, "I want you to know that as a wedding present I am recommending you for field promotion to captain." When the steward filled the glasses again, the general added, "Now we drink to all the rest who nobly aided these two in their important mission to Fort Mahone. Neither must we forget the gallant vessel herself—Captain Munro's great lady! *Rose of Dundee!*"

They drank, and cheered, and pounded the table.

"Eh?" the general asked, bending to listen to a yellow-chevroned sergeant who sidled through the doorway, hat in hand. "What's that, soldier?"

The man repeated his whispered message. General Terry stroked his beard, looked concerned. Rollo Gamble, holding Nora's hand, asked, "Sir, what is it?"

The general put down his glass.

"Rose of Dundee," he announced, "has sunk at her moorings. The men worked hard to save her, but apparently she sprang a massive leak and went down in a hurry. Only her upper works are sticking out."

Chapter Twelve

General Alfred Terry's expedition, the third prong of the campaign against the warlike Sioux, was moving out. Alec paid no attention to the line of mounted cavalrymen, the blue army wagons, the flying pennons. Instead, he sat on the riverbank in misty rain, staring at the wreckage of *Rose of Dundee*'s pilothouse, all that showed above the rain-pocked waters of the Yellowstone.

Almost uncaring, he clutched in one hand the five hundred dollars in greenbacks Rollo Gamble had paid him. Rosie had earned that money—in fact, had given her life for it. Now what did the moist bills mean? Nothing, except perhaps to pay off Nora's loan, and Sam Fat and Hugh Munro, and maybe to give a little grubstake to Woolly Willie Yates and Frenchy Villard. Ben Bagley was a peace officer, however. To attempt to recompense Ben for his help would be interpreted as bribery, in addition to all the other charges against Alec Munro.

After a while the end of the column disappeared from view. The day was green and soft and misty, hillsides mantled in pastel velvet. Pepperpot and Solomon Two, rescued from a watery grave by the army detail, grazed peacefully near the river. Alec was wet through but hardly cared. Maybe he would catch lung fever and die a tragic death. Lung fever, with a wasted body and feverish brow, was preferable to spending the rest of his life in jail. He took off his sodden coat and tattered uniform cap, hoping thereby to hasten the onset of the disease. At any moment Horace Tobin's *Sultan* might steam up to the Fort Mahone landing and his career as a lightning pilot would come to an end.

Deep in reverie, he became aware of bells ringing from the post chapel. Nora was going to be married this morning, married to Lieutenant—no, Captain—Captain Rollo Gamble, USA. Wearily he squashed the packet of bills into his pocket and limped to his feet. Although his ankle was still swollen and hurt like blazes he had discarded the crutch, preferring to meet his fate on two legs. He did not want to go to any wedding this morning, especially Nora Tobin's wedding. But there were courtesies to be observed, and he was an old friend; that, and only that.

The chapel was a small building of rough-sawn pine boards. In the pews sat Uncle Hugh Munro, uncomfortable in celluloid collar and dingy black coat with the elbows out. Willie Yates was there also, along with Ben Bagley and Frenchy Villard and Sam Fat. The rest of the chapel was filled with army officers, probably friends of the groom. The chaplain, wearing a white surplice and a beatific smile, met Alec at the door.

"Captain Munro, glad to meet you. I understand you're a friend of the bride."

"You could say that, I guess," Alec answered gloomily.

He sat beside his uncle.

"You're late, boyo," Hugh whispered.

"I got to thinking about it and decided I might as well show her I don't give a damn who she marries!"

"Foosh!" Hugh snorted.

"Nevertheless—"

"Hush, now! The ceremonies is starting!"

Nora was radiantly beautiful, though a trifle pale. Mrs. Stockdale had loaned Nora her own wedding gown, and stood up with her. The best man was a lanky engineer officer, a friend of Rollo Gamble's. Nora had talked Ben Bagley into giving her away. Ben was doubtful of the propriety of the arrangement, but Nora pointed out that the sheriff had known her since she was a little girl and owed her that. She always got her way, Alec remembered, though usually in some oblique feminine manner.

Rollo Gamble was resplendent in dress blues, the carefully brushed Kossuth hat under his good arm, the corps badge shining. His moustache bristled; the long-unkempt hair was freshly barbered and gleamed with pomade. In spite of himself Alec had to admit that Rollo cut a handsome figure, even with his arm in a sling.

"They *both* look pale," he muttered to Hugh.

"Marriage," his uncle said, "is a solemn occasion, like a hanging."

"Friends—" the chaplain began, beaming over his pince-nez, "we are gathered here today to—"

Alec didn't hear the rest. His mind began to wander. Into his mind's eye came unbidden a photographic image of a day in June, just a year ago. He and Nora drifted in *Rose of Dundee*'s dinghy on the waters of Wicket's Branch. Nora had not yet gone away to finishing school in Omaha. With a pang he remembered the straw hat, the flowered dress, Nora's slender fingers trailing in the water. He rowed, covertly watching from under the visor of his captain's cap. *Nora*, he sighed. *Ah, Nora!*

"Stop blowing like a grampus!" Uncle Hugh muttered. "You're disturbing the ceremonies!"

In spite of himself he fell again into the reverie. He saw her face on that golden day in June, her bare brown arms. He remembered the lazy buzzing of the bees, the lapping waters. Old Horace did not know where his daughter had gone; Nora had put on her prettiest frock and sneaked out to join Alec. His mind remembered the picture: the softly shaded face under the hat, downcast blue eyes, the captivating cleft in her chin. A wave of nostalgia overcame him. God worked in mysterious ways, the Presbyterian deity most of all.

"Eh?" He looked up again, startled. Hugh Munro glowered at him. Other spectators turned in their seats, frowning.

"Stop that infernal whistling!"

"I wasn't whistling!"

"You were too! That pap about a blue-eyed daisy or whatever it was!"

Alec felt himself blushing. "I'm sorry," he apologized, and tried to smile at the guests.

"Well!" the chaplain said, clearing his throat. He took a glass of water from the lectern. "Now where was I?"

Alec closed his eyes in silent misery, a knife twisting in his bosom. He should not have come; he was only embarrassing people. Still, there it was! Rosie, the old flame who was going to comfort him in his declining years, was gone. Alec Munro was abandoned in the world, a plaything of fate, buffeted and scorned.

"If there be any man here—"

Still, he could not go down to defeat this way. He was a Scot, and a Munro on top of that.

"—who knows why these two—"

Resolve hardened within him. In spite of insuperable obstacles he had brought *Rose of Dundee* upriver in boiling floods, delivering her cargo on time in spite of Indian attacks, mutiny, and shipwreck.

"—should not be joined together—"

He stood up.

"—in the bonds of holy matrimony—"

Someone spoke, loudly. "I do!"

There was a shocked silence. The chaplain adjusted his pince-nez. "Ah—what's that?"

Alec realized that he was the one who had spoken out.

"I do!" he repeated.

The chaplain was puzzled. "Young man, you do *what?*"

"I know someone—that is, I mean to say—"

Behind him someone chuckled. "Go to it, boyo!" his uncle muttered.

"I mean I know someone that knows a reason why these two should not be joined together in the bonds of holy matrimony or whatever you said. That's what you asked, didn't you?"

The chaplain's mouth opened and closed but no sound came out. "I say, now!" Rollo Gamble protested, stepping forward. "This is too much! After all—"

"I mean me," Alec said firmly. *"I'm* the one that knows why they shouldn't be joined or whatever. The reason is that Miss Tobin loves me, not Rollo Gamble! She has loved me for several years now, though sometimes she has funny ways of showing it. Maybe I haven't always been worthy of that love, either, but it's just plain inconceivable she should marry anyone else!"

Nora stared at him curiously. "Alec Munro, are you crazy?"

"You know what I say is true, Nora Tobin! You're just trying to make me jealous, that's all! For a long time I didn't understand. But now the scales have fallen from my eyes and I see the truth."

"Alec—" Gamble said.

"I'm awfully sorry about this, Rollo! You're a good man. I like you a lot. But this match is wrong for you, wrong for Nora. I guess we'd better call off the marriage—this *particular* marriage, I mean!"

Rollo's face reddened; his moustaches flared. "Goddamnit—excuse me, Father—you can't just come barging in here and take over a man's marriage! What kind of a fool do you think I am?"

"You're not a fool, Rollo," Alec said kindly. "You're just misguided, that's all. I can understand, you know. Nora is a very confusing person sometimes. But believe me—"

"Wait a minute!" Nora snapped.

They waited.

"Why doesn't someone notice I'm here? It sounds to me like you two are haggling over a female slave at an auction!"

"That's right!" Rollo protested. He tried to take Nora's arm but she jerked away; he looked surprised, and hurt. "Nora!" he said plaintively.

"She's going to talk," Alec said. "When she's going to talk, there's naught for it but to let her. I found that out a long time ago!"

Nora stared at him, lips set. "You, Alec Munro," she announced, "are a crude and boorish man! How dare you disrupt my marriage to Lieutenant—I mean Captain Gamble?"

"Because I love you and he doesn't! He's just dazzled a little, but when that wears off you'll need someone that understands you—like I do."

"What do you mean—dazzled?"

"What I meant, Nora, is that my love—the love of Alec Munro—is the enduring kind—the kind that's gone through fire and flood and female vapors and still endures, green and fresh as the banks of Loch Tay."

"You're just saying that!"

Alec held up his hand. "On the bones of John Knox, I swear it!"

"I never heard you talk like that before! You always seemed tongue-tied when I spoke of love."

He shrugged. "I was a slow starter, Nora. It takes a Scot a little time to get ready. We're a cautious race, you know. But now I'm set. With a little practice I can probably turn a phrase with the best of them, though I don't speak French and I never was to college."

Nora appeared confused. She looked down at her bouquet. "This is all so sudden. I can't—"

"Of course you can! Look—this has been just a rehearsal up to this point! Now we can get on to the genuine article!"

The engineer officer spoke up. "For God's sake, Rollo, speak up! You're a lawyer—don't you see this man is taking title to your bride?"

"No one," Nora said, "has title to me!"

Rollo looked faint. "But I thought—I mean—I understood we had an understanding!"

Nora pursed her lips thoughtfully. "Well, Alec's got a point, you know! He's awful dim-witted and slow, but he's got the Scots knack of muddling about till he gropes his way clear."

Rollo's eyes glazed. "You mean—"

"I'm afraid I don't quite understand all this," the chaplain said. "Is there or is there not a marriage to be performed here today?"

"I don't doubt he's right—in the long run, I mean. He's such an old stick-in-the-mud, and you were so dashing and gallant, Rollo. It quite turned my head."

Gamble continued to stand transfixed, eyes resembling those of a stuffed owl. The Kossuth hat dropped from beneath his arm and Nora knelt to pick it up.

"Now about the other marriage," Alec said, turning to the chaplain. "Does your master's license or whatever it's called let you marry civilians? I mean, like me?"

The chaplain poured himself another glass of water. His hand trembled and much of the water went on the floor.

"In twenty-three years as an army chaplain I never—"

The engineer officer hissed in Rollo's ear. "Damn it, man, you're being outflanked! Protect your rear!"

"But you could marry us?" Alec insisted.

Dazed, the chaplain nodded. "I guess so. But I don't know what the commandant will say."

Mrs. Stockdale spoke. "Pish!"

"Eh?"

"Henry hasn't got anything to say about it! If there has been some mix-up, and these are really the people that love each other, then it's your duty to marry them, Chaplain!" She turned to Rollo Gamble, who was perspiring heavily. "Captain Gamble, you'll just have to take your lumps! It wouldn't be the first time a man has been stood up at the altar. I stood up one myself before I married Henry Stockdale!"

Ignoring the others, Alec approached Nora, who eyed him askance. Stiffly, because of his bad ankle, he got to his knees. "Nora Tobin," he said with simple dignity, "I'll probably go to jail when your pa's *Sultan* gets here. My boat's sunk, and my sprained ankle hurts like the dickens. I have no prospects, nothing to recommend me, except I'm in love with you. I was in love with you the first day I ever saw you and I never stopped, even when you were selfish and mean. But that's all in the past now. Will you marry me?"

Thoughtfully Nora plucked petals from the wilting bouquet. At last she looked at him.

"You really mean all you said? About loving me that first day and ever since?"

"I do."

"It's not just a figure of speech?"

"It comes from the heart!"

She took a deep breath; her bosom rose and fell with emotion. Some of the petals of the bouquet fell off.

"Damn it all," Alec protested, "if you're playing 'he loves me—he loves me not' . . ."

"Shut up!" Uncle Hugh hissed in his ear.

Nora looked at Captain Gamble. "Here's your hat," she said, handing it over.

"Eh?"

"I guess it's all clear to me too now, Rollo. I must go where my heart tells me." She turned to Alec. "Get up! You look foolish down there!" She took his arm in hers, face shining. "Yes, I'll marry you, Alec Munro!"

There was bedlam. Uncle Hugh Munro led the applause of the late *Rose of Dundee*'s crew. Rollo Gamble's military friends crowded sympathetically around him, all talking at once, but he shook them off, looking warlike. A muttered conference ensued, and Rollo approached Alec, the best man at his side.

"Rollo," Alec said, "I know how these things are done." He glanced at the engineer officer. "I guess this gentleman is your second."

Gamble looked puzzled.

"Anyway," Alec continued, "I'm the one challenged, so I get the choice of weapons. I was never a very good shot, but I'm fair with the claymore and dirk. As soon as your arm heals—"

The engineer officer looked startled. "He thinks it's a duel you want, Rollo!"

Gamble grimaced. "That's not it at all! I—I just wanted to say—" He broke off, stumbling for words. The quick and incisive manner had vanished. He mopped his forehead with a clean folded handkerchief. "Damn it all, I mean to say it's probably for the best! You're right—Nora loves you. Even when I was making calf's-eyes at her on the boat I suspected she'd never lose hope you'd speak up, claim her." Moustaches drooping, he stared into his hat. "I've always had an eye for the ladies. Nora's the most beautiful I ever saw. You're right—I was dazzled, and against my better judgment."

"What does that mean, Rollo?" Nora asked quickly.

"No offense, Nora! I just meant that for a little while I forgot I was a bachelor. I wasn't ever serious, even when I thought I was. I'd have brought you sorrow and pain, Nora, in spite of myself. So we've both got Alec to thank for saving us from ourselves." Again he hesitated, consulted the interior of his hat. "I thank you for the experience, ma'am. I know you and Alec will be very happy, no matter what happens with Mr. Tobin and Captain Winkle."

The engineer officer clapped him on the back. "Spoke like a soldier, Rollo! Now let's have a drink!"

The vibration of a whistle shook the resinous boards of the chapel. Horace Tobin's *Sultan*—Captain Julius Winkle, master —had finally arrived at Fort Mahone. They all ran to the window to look. *Sultan* was only the second vessel to come upstream since the June rise. A vapor of steam issued from the big boat's polished brass whistle. A moment later the windows of the chapel rattled with the deep blast.

"That's *Sultan*, all right," Alec murmured. "I didn't think she'd be far behind."

"Whatever will we do, Alec?" Nora asked.

Ben Bagley cleared his throat. "Alec, I got to arrest you. Old Horace will want to see you in irons at least. But you won't let the cat out of the bag about disarming me with Miss Nora's valise?"

"Of course not."

"Nothing personal in this, you understand. I got my duty as sheriff, same as you did as master of poor old Rosie."

Nora, clutching the tattered bouquet, leaned forward to kiss Rollo Gamble on the cheek. Some of the color had returned to his face. "Rollo," she said in a husky voice, "I'll always remember you! Our first child may very well be named 'Alec Rollo Munro!'"

Ben Bagley took Alec's arm. "I see Winkle and old Horace on the dock already. We better get down there."

Alec shrugged. "You always get your man, Ben." To Nora he whispered, "You sure you don't want to back out? This is your last chance!"

She kissed him, but with considerably more physicality than she had expended on Rollo Gamble. "Dear Alec, what would I be without you? From now on you may expect me to be always at your side!"

Old Horace was leaning on his umbrella, Captain Julius Winkle beside him, as the little party walked out on the Fort Mahone landing. The new arrivals were inspecting the wreckage of the late independent, *Rose of Dundee,* with glee. When Horace saw Ben he yelled.

"Put the cuffs on him, Ben! Don't let the scoundrel get away! He's dangerous!"

Julius Winkle, sleek in gold braid and high starched collar, rushed to meet Nora Tobin. "My dear, you're safe!" Sternly he turned to Alec Munro. "Has this scoundrel harmed you?" He tried to take Nora's hand, but she pushed him away.

"Nora!" he protested. "It's me—Julius—your betrothed! Whatever has happened to you?" He turned to Horace. "I fear this experience has unhinged the girl's mind!"

"Pooh!" Nora snapped. "I'm not your betrothed!"

"But—"

"I'm not your anything! And if anyone's mind is unhinged, it's yours, Julius Winkle!"

When Winkle again tried to take her hand, Alec stepped forward and seized the captain's coat, loosening a few brass buttons. "Stop bothering her, Winkle!"

"I told you!" Horace shrilled, shaking his umbrella. "He's a lunatic, Ben! Put the cuffs on him!"

Winkle stared at Nora's wedding attire, seeming to notice it for the first time. "Is that—don't tell me—you're not going to marry—" He seemed to choke. "Alec Munro kidnapped you, bore you away screaming and struggling from your father's house!"

"That's right!" Horace confirmed. "Like the rape of the Sabine women in the Bible! Come in the night, he did, to snatch her from a loving father! I tell you, the man is an instrument of Satan!"

Nora handed Alec her bouquet and put her hands on her hips.

"Let's get this straight," she said firmly. "Alec didn't kidnap me at all! I wasn't sure I loved Julius, so I had Bessie pack my valise and I stowed away on Alec Munro's *Rose of Dundee* to visit Aunt Belle Goggins at Turkey Flats. I was distraught, and needed time to think. Aunt Belle was always kind to me, understood me, so I wanted to ask her advice before such a fateful decision."

Julius Winkle wet his lips, leaned forward. "But—"

"I don't love you, Julius! I'm sorry, but that's the way it is! You're a very—well, a very *interesting* man in lots of ways. But that's no basis for a marriage, is it now?"

Winkle paled. "There's chicanery afoot here!"

"Shut up, Julius," Horace snapped. He sidled near Nora, giving Alec Munro a wide berth. "What is this frippery you've got on then, daughter? It looks to me like a wedding dress."

"It is."

Rollo Gamble spoke up. "Nora was going to marry me, sir." Horace looked at him in surprise, one woolly eyebrow cocked, the other sagging over a malevolent eye. "Who the hell are you?"

"Lieutenant—I beg your pardon—Captain Rollo P. Gamble, USA."

Horace nodded. "I remember you! You were that cheeky jackanapes wanted me to ship your traps up to Fort Mahone in a raging flood!"

"That's right, sir. But on the trip Miss Tobin and I became friendly. Nora is a beautiful woman, and could charm the birds out of the trees. The nuptials are—were—set for this morning. But—"

"Then I got here just in time!" Horace crowed. "I'll not have my daughter wed an Army man! I'll not let her marry into the damned Army and leave me alone in my old age while she goes gallivanting off to Texas or Florida or God knows where!"

"I wasn't going to marry Rollo anyway!" Nora snapped.

"Then why are you dressed up like that?"

Feeling it time he entered the conversation, Alec spoke as a prospective son-in-law. "Because," he explained, "when it came time for Nora to take her vows, I put my oar in and told Nora she didn't love Rollo Gamble either. I could see what was happening. Nora wanted to love someone, to be a good wife to someone, but she was just a little confused. So I spoke up and explained how she loved me, not Rollo."

Horace paled, staggered as if struck by a rattler. "You? Not —not Alec Munro!"

Nora put her arm firmly in Alec's. "That's right, Father! It took a little time to make up my mind, but I'm going to marry Alec!"

"She's all dressed for it anyway," Alec pointed out, "and there won't be any additional expense. We can even use the same flowers."

Julius Winkle protested. "But he's a jailbird! Sheriff Bagley, you heard what Mr. Tobin said! Put the cuffs on him! Munro's wanted for unlawfully taking possession of an impounded vessel. That's a federal crime! Five thousand dollars and five years in jail!"

Alec fumbled in his pocket and counted out greenbacks. "Here," he said, holding out the money to Horace Tobin. "Three hundred and fifty dollars! Mr. Tobin, that's what I owe you for the repairs your marine works did on *Rose of Dundee.*"

Horace drew back. "Too late! You committed a federal crime, like Julius says! I'd be aiding and abetting a felony if I was to take your money now!" He shook the umbrella. "Ben, how many times I got to tell you to put the cuffs on that lawbreaker?"

"You can't put him in jail!" Nora protested. "Father, please! Alec is the man I want to marry!"

"You ain't married yet, are you?"

"No, but—"

"Then you ain't going to be married, daughter, especially to no criminal like Alec Munro!"

Ben Bagley produced a pair of manacles. "Alec," he said, "I'm sorry about this, but I got a sworn duty to perform."

"What about him?" Alec glowered at Julius Winkle. "He rammed *Rose of Dundee,* didn't he? It was a miracle we didn't go to the bottom after he tried to cut us in two!"

Captain Winkle smiled an oily smile. "A failure," he said, "of the engine room bells. The cable broke, you see. I was unable to ring down the engines when we came off the bar."

"That's a fine story!" Alec snorted. Fists doubled, he started toward Julius Winkle, who quickly took cover behind Ben Bagley.

"Come on, Alec!" the sheriff urged, holding out the manacles. "I don't like this any better than you do, but I got to do it!"

Tenderly Alec kissed Nora. He had kissed her once before, in a kind of glancing way, but this was different. "I guess it's all over," he sighed. "I'm sorry, Nora. I'll always love you, even within the gray walls of my prison cell."

"Wait a minute," someone suggested.

Alec turned. Rollo Gamble, seeming fully restored, strolled forward, fondling his moustaches. He and his engineer friend had followed the little group down to the landing. "I had an idea that I might come in handy about this time," he said.

Horace Tobin objected. "There's been too much palavering already!" he snarled. "I got to get downriver in a hurry! Business matters!"

"This is business too," Rollo said.

They stared at him with interest but without much hope— Nora, Alec, Uncle Hugh Munro, Sam Fat, Willie Yates, Frenchy Villard.

"I was a lawyer in Boston before I gave up private practice to enlist in the War. Later, I was in the Judge Advocate General's office, adjudicating claims. That was before I volunteered for duty out here on the frontier, and was posted to Fort Van Buren. This isn't the story of my life. It's just to prove I know something about the law, especially maritime law. Now Mr. Tobin's vessel *Sultan* was in great distress on that bar when you pulled her off, Alec. Isn't that true?"

Puzzled, Alec nodded. "She was about to go to pieces!"

There was a chorus of confirmation from Hugh, Willie, and the rest. "That's a fact!" "Busted pipes shooting steam all over the place!" "Hog chains snapped like wet noodles!" "I'd have give her three minutes more, and that's all!"

"Now wait a minute!" Captain Winkle protested. "We were about to get off under our own power!"

"What's this all about?" Horace demanded.

"Just this." Rollo was cool, lawyerlike. "*Sultan* was in dire peril. There are many witnesses who can testify to that. Alec Munro's *Rose of Dundee* pulled *Sultan* off, saving the vessel, any cargo, and possibly the lives of those aboard. Furthermore, he did so at the peril of his own vessel. *Rose of Dundee* was leaking badly and in danger of her boiler blowing up because of the effort of towing *Sultan* with such a small vessel."

"That's true!" Uncle Hugh confirmed, ruffling his short-cropped curls with his fingers. "Look at all these new white hairs!"

"Therefore," Gamble went on, "Captain Munro may now legally bring forth a claim *in personam,* as we lawyers say, against the owners of *Sultan*—namely, Missouri Packet Lines and Horace Tobin—or *in rem,* as we further say, against *Sultan;* that is to say, a claim against *Sultan* herself. If a favorable judgment issues from federal court, as I do not doubt it will, *Sultan* can be sold by order of the court to satisfy Captain Munro's legitimate salvage claim."

Horace Tobin's woolly brows drew together. "That's just a lot of guff! You're trying to scare me out of my lawful prosecution of this rascal Munro!"

In spite of his late marital disappointment, Captain Gamble seemed to be enjoying himself. "You may very well be scared, sir. The least you can look forward to is a protracted proceeding in court, with *Sultan* and other assets of Missouri Packet Lines tied up by injunction until the case is decided!"

Alec spoke in low tones to Rollo. "I haven't got money for a lawyer!"

"That's all right," Rollo grinned. "I'm on sick leave from the Army till these blasted ribs heal! I'll take the case for nothing, just to keep my hand in!"

Winkle dabbed at his face with a handkerchief. Balefully he pointed to Willie Yates, Frenchy Villard, Sam Fat, the rest. "This bunch of blackguards will swear to it in court, though I still think we could have got off under our own power if—"

"If!" Horace barked. "Goddamnit, if the Yellowstone River was full of sorghum molasses, I wouldn't have to pay twenty cents a quart to pour it on my flapjacks of a morning! If! If! You're an idiot, Winkle—a blithering idiot! I don't know why I ever thought I wanted my little Nora to marry you!"

Winkle flushed. "Damn it, you old crook, you're in this just as deep as me! When I wanted to ram *Rose of Dundee* to stop her from getting away, you said 'all right.' You said, 'I wanted that pesky Munro's boat, but maybe it's better to send her to the bottom where she won't steal any more freight from me.' That's exactly what you said!"

"I don't remember any such thing!" Horace said hastily. "Anyway, that's in the past! Now we got to decide about this salvage thing, and you're as much help as a case of smallpox!" Uneasily he pulled at his beard, ground the tip of the umbrella into the spongy boards of the dock.

"Captain Gamble's right," the engineer officer remarked. "Rollo and I practiced law in the same office in Boston, and there isn't much he doesn't know about the laws governing salvage. He's a cagey lawyer, too—he could get a judgment for the Emperor Nero for fire damage to his fiddle!"

"Not only that," Nora exclaimed, "but I'm going to marry Alec if I have to do it behind bars! So there!" She tossed her head; the taffy curls flounced. "I love him!"

"I give up!" Horace howled, raising fists above his head. "Damn it all, I know when I'm licked!" He pounded the umbrella into the planks of the dock and the shaft broke. "Ben, can I just drop the charges against—" Words failed him. He indicated Alec Munro. "Against—him."

"My name," Alec said, "is Alec McKenzie Munro. You'd better get used to it, Pa!"

Horace's face turned mottled red. Frustrated, he threw the mangled umbrella into the river. Wrathfully he stared at Julius Winkle. "As for you, Winkle, after this you couldn't captain a canoe for me! This wild-goose chase was your idea! Get out of my sight before I throw you into the river after my umbrella!"

Alec shook hands with Rollo Gamble. "You're a brick," he said, "to do all this for me—for us—after I stole your girl away."

"Maybe I still love her," Gamble said. "But I guess I'll get used to it."

This time Horace Tobin unwillingly gave his daughter away, mumbling to himself. Rollo Gamble stood up with Alec.

As the happy couple left the chapel in the June sunshine, Gamble turned to Hugh Munro.

"What in hell is that tune Alec's whistling? Seems to me I heard it a lot on the boat."

Alec's uncle grinned. " 'My True Love Is a Blue-eyed Daisy.' And Alec finally come to bloom too!"

Epilogue

Old Horace Tobin, "fair caught," as he admitted, gave command of *Sultan* to his new son-in-law. Horace eventually became a doting grandfather to little Alec Rollo Munro.

Captain Gamble remained a bachelor until he died. Going back to the practice of law, he became a highly respected justice of the Supreme Court of the Commonwealth of Massachusetts.

Julius Winkle left the river in disgrace. He was last heard of running a brothel in San Francisco.

Uncle Hugh Munro married Nora Tobin's Aunt Belle. Midway between Fort Mahone and Turkey Flats he opened a saloon called "The Cock of the North," catering both to soldiers and civilians.

Woolly Willie Yates, tiring of his former violent life, enlisted as farrier at Fort Mahone, giving for recommendation the fact that he had once been a blacksmith in Chillicothe, Missouri.

In spite of his wounded shoulder, Frenchy Villard volunteered to ride with General Terry's column as a scout. Far in advance of the column, he was the first to discover the fate of Lt. Col. George Armstrong Custer and his men. Later he was awarded a medal for his services, and eventually went back to woodhawking on the river.

Sam Fat, though offered a berth on *Sultan*, decided mudclerking on the river was too strenuous. He opened a moderately successful laundry near Fort Mahone. He, Willie Yates, and Hugh Munro sat frequently on the Goggins veranda in Turkey Flats discussing old times on the river.

Ben Bagley retired to wed the Widow McKeever in Springer's Landing. He eventually became a deacon of the church. A great friend of children, he told them many stories, but never revealed how Alec Munro once disarmed him with a lady's valise.

In 1883 Fort Mahone was abandoned. All activities were moved to Fort Abraham Lincoln in the Dakota Territory. In 1921 a party of surveyors, setting a stake for reference purposes, discovered on the site of the old post the ancient brass nameplate from an early Yellowstone paddle-wheeler. The plate was too corroded to read with certainty, but the surveyors notified Dr. George K. Millwright, famous Western archaeologist. Dr. Millwright brought in student aides who dug up timbers, spars, and a portion of an oak ship's wheel, well preserved in the swampy bottomland along the river. No identification could be made of the vessel.

Dr. Millwright, examining a fragment of deck planking, was struck by the fact that even at that late date, forty or fifty years after the nameless vessel sank, a mysterious odor still emanated from the specimen.

"If I didn't know better," he remarked to one of his Archaeology III students, a youth named Homer Bibberman, "I'd say it was scotch whisky!"